Acclaim for Michael Winter's

One Last Good Look

"Winter has an unerring ear for dialogue, for its starts and stutters and serpentine ellipses, and for dialect — in this case, [Newfoundland's] inhabitants' sardonic, obliquely twisted humour, their dense, earthy vernacular. He's also blessed with an elegant, assured sense of rhythm, topped off with a kinetic, vital prose, with precise imagery that jars delightfully. All this without stooping to cloying folksiness. Although the stories in this collection function perfectly well as autonomous, discrete units, as a whole they provide a cogent, complex portrait of one individual's passage into adulthood. Highly recommended."

— GLOBE AND MAIL

"Michael Winter's [*One Last Good Look*] is, finally, a book I can rhapsodize and wax lyrical about without resorting to dodgy euphemisms. Winter's ruthlessly austere style — think early Hemingway or Carver, stripped to an even further minimized minimalism — slyly packs in layers of emotional nuance, complexity and ambiguity. . . . These are superb stories: subtle, wise, and faultlessly realistic. Sorry, no picturesque descriptions of dust motes swimming in refracted sunbeams. Just fresh insights into human nature worth pondering."

— TORONTO STAR

"Winter's writing is particularly mesmerizing when he illustrates [the] troubled yet affectionate bond between Gabriel and June. It is this bond, a tangled web of tension and love, that is at the core of the two best stories in this collection. . . . exemplary and provocative writing."

— WINNIPEG FREE PRESS

"[Winter's protagonist] Gabriel English may not be, as his biblical namesake, a messenger of God, but he is a virtuous and obliging lad and he is touched by light. . . . there is little that Gabriel doesn't notice. His observations of the smallest detail are stunning throughout the book. Each small section presents an image as tangible as a photograph as the chapters wind, sometimes linearly, sometimes a mix of past and present, through the rites of his life."

— ATLANTIC BOOKS TODAY

"Michael Winter's *One Last Good Look* is a deftly written collection of connected short stories. . . . This is writing of a distilled essence, where a brief interpolated description of Mom making tomato relish suggests something about the denial, the miscommunication, and the anguish of a family not functioning as smoothly as it should. . . . *One Last Good Look* is like a photo album of snapshots of people you don't know, but as you flip through its leaves, you recognize faces, expressions, and postures that enable you to imagine what those people might be like."

— WINNIPEG *UPTOWN*

"*One Last Good Look* is an ironic reference to [protagonist] Gabe English's inability to settle on a place, a woman, an allegiance, a narrative line or form. . . . Such formal tomfoolery accounts for much of the book's tempting beauty. . . . English is irresistible: wit, grief, sexuality, intellect and an alluring habit of speech that leaves so much out. *One Last Good Look* . . . asks that we read well and acutely, give ourselves over to his style, drift into the gaps."

— *MALAHAT REVIEW*

"What I particularly like about Winter's writing is his sense of the absurd . . . Humour has often been all too absent in Canadian fiction. This situation is starting to change, thankfully, and Winter has made a contribution. His quick, clipped dialogue has the ring of the real because he has clearly spent time listening to the voices around him . . . His sentences sting like fingernails clipped too close . . . Winter manages to infuse crisis with humour, which is a subtle balancing act from a fine and penetrating writer."

— *EVENT*

"*One Last Good Look* is an assured collection. . . . Throughout all his trials, Gabriel remains an engaging protagonist. The most important character in the stories, however, is Newfoundland itself. Whether through dialogue, description of people or landscape, the Newfoundland that emerges in *One Last Good Look* is authentic and wholly convincing."

— *KITCHENER RECORD*

One

Last Good Look

One
Last Good Look

Michael Winter

This edition published in 2001 by
House of Anansi Press Limited
895 Don Mills Road
400-2 Park Centre
Toronto, ON M3C 1W3
Tel. (416) 445-3333
Fax (416) 445-5967
www.anansi.ca

First published in 1999 by The Porcupine's Quill

Distributed in Canada by
General Distribution Services Ltd.
325 Humber College Blvd.
Etobicoke, ON M9W 7C3
Tel. (416) 213-1919
Fax (416) 213-1917
E-mail cservice@genpub.com

Distributed in the United States by
General Distribution Services Inc.
PMB 128, 4500 Witmer Industrial Estates
Niagara Falls, NY 14305-1386
Toll Free Tel. 1-800-805-1083
Toll Free Fax 1-800-481-6207
E-mail gdsinc@genpub.com

04 03 02 01 00   1 2 3 4 5

CANADIAN CATALOGUING IN PUBLICATION DATA

Winter, Michael Hardy, 1965–
One last good look
ISBN 0-88784-667-X

I. Title.

PS8595.I623O53 2001   C813'.54   C00-933187-5
PR9199.3.W56O53 2001

Cover design: Bill Douglas @ The Bang
Typesetting: Brian Panhuyzen
Printed and bound in Canada

THE CANADA COUNCIL | LE CONSEIL DES ARTS
FOR THE ARTS | DU CANADA
SINCE 1957 | DEPUIS 1957

*We acknowledge for their financial support of our publishing program the Canada Council for the
Arts, the Ontario Arts Council, and the Government of Canada through the Book Publishing
Industry Development Program (BPIDP).*

for

MAM, DAD, KATHLEEN, PAUL

I would like to thank the Canada Council, the Newfoundland and Labrador Arts Council, and the St John's City Arts Jury, for their financial support during the writing of this book.

I am grateful to members of the Burning Rock who listened to, and commented on, various forms of this book over the past five years. I thank Claire Wilkshire, Larry Mathews, Lisa Moore and Mary Lewis for reading the final manuscript and suggesting many critical improvements which I could no longer ignore.

— *M. W.*

Contents

All the new thinking is about loss.
In this it resembles all the old thinking.
— *Robert Hass*

Something Practical

Gabriel English was refinishing furniture that summer for Andrew Hall in Curling. He learned how to french polish from Mr Hall, who had been resettled from Woods Island and used to build boats. Gabriel's hands were stiff with shellac and sore from the gestetner duplicating fluid Mr Hall used to strip old finishes. Gabriel met Doris Parsons when he was delivering a sideboard to an old woman in Mount Moriah. Mr Hall was in charge and Gabriel his helper. Andrew Hall called the woman Nan Brennan, and she said, Those kids got my rhubarb all tore up, Andrew. Next time I sees them I'll get my axe out and clean them. And Doris Parsons came downstairs and said hello to Andrew — she called him by his first name — and Andrew said Hello Doris and she looked at Gabriel. She helped Nan Brennan with the money which was kept in a breadbox behind a loaf and Andrew Hall thanked them both.

Nan Brennan was wearing a baseball cap that had a wool pom-pom and her T-shirt was an advertisement for running shoes.

Mr Hall, in the truck, said Doris Parsons left her family up Elizabeth Avenue and is living with her Nan, and he saw how Gabriel was looking at her and he should know that Doris is seeing a fellow, name of Hector Abbott, who was a high school wrestler but had a hole in his heart.

Gabriel knew of Hector Abbott and thought it appropriate for them to be going out. He saw Doris at the mall next.

She said, It's very hard to be yourself and it's just as hard to know what you want, isnt it?

She said she just loves these shoes in Agnew but they werent getting any cheaper and she could laugh at her own wants but nothing could deny that she'd love to have them.

You know what, she said. You could wear better jeans. Those jeans are all wrong.

She took him to the Bay and waded through racks of pants. These, she said. Try these.

Gabriel came out in the pants and they werent right but she knew where to go from there and he knew where she was going and he helped her pick out the pair.

Those, she said, are gorgeous on you.

And they werent that expensive. Doris had gone to a sale rack.

She invited him down to Mount Moriah and he offered her a ride. Gabriel was a new driver in his father's car. He liked driving a standard. He said of french polishing the trick is to use a dab of oil and to spirit it off at the end. Doris said she'd like to see that, that she loves tricks.

Nan Brennan was watching city workers shovel pieces of pavement off the road. She raps on the window: Youre swiping my pavement! A worker tilts his hard hat at her.

Doris: What do you think of me living with her.

A girl who can have the rooms upstairs, Nan says. I never set foot up there. Hello, she says to Gabriel.

There's a vinegar plant below the stair. When Nan understands that Gabriel is interested, she peels a few layers of the mother into a jar with some of the liquor. Nobody cares about all this, she says. It's vinyl siding and aluminum boats and they'll steal the road right out from under you.

Theyre recycling, Nan, Doris says. Theyre gonna put back your road.

That road is gone now, Doris. The new council will come in and we'll lose the ward and that fellow from Humber Heights will see I never get a decent road.

And she might be right at that.

Gabriel thinks: You are in my bones as deep as radiation.

Doris telephones him because he is shy and she says this, I'd never see you again if I didnt call and Gabriel admits to this and she says I like that about you, that you admit to things. They walk up Crow Hill as the sun sinks over the Bay of Islands. He has to push on the tops of his knees. The height makes Weebald a black stone in the sea. There is a monument Gabriel has never read, praising Cook.

Doris: This city is some new.

That mill used to be the largest on earth.

How can it not be largest now?

Gabriel: Like Everest not being the biggest. Theyve found mountains in the sea.

The rocks are old, she said.

How do you know.

They date it. It's some of the oldest rock on earth.

How can you tell what's old?

They measure it against things.

Gabriel: But if it's oldest. What do you measure it against?

The newer things.

Blue rock drops sheer to the shore road. You can fall clear for a hundred feet. Gabriel knows the height because the public library is ten storeys and where they stand is greater. His best marks are in geography but he never knew about the oldest rock. Doris leans over at the road below, the pulp mill and the yard of spruce logs. They were still driving logs down the Humber. Mr Hall had said all this will change. Transport trucks will take over from the rivers. The air absorbed in yellow sulphur. In the mornings the hoods of cars covered in a blond ash like yeast flakes. Dumped bark forming a peninsula in the bay, pointing north like a gloved finger.

They should have a guardrail.

You can measure it with a jump.

Doris.

A jump off the oldest rock on earth. I want to jump on the largest mill on earth.

Dont be joking.

She turns and lifts her wrists as if to say, dont worry.

Theyre at the same height as Elizabeth Avenue where her parents live and her twin brothers at the rim of Corner Brook. Gabriel spent last summer building a house up there with his father but he never saw Doris and she said she was still up there then though she didnt spend much time there.

A red glow of a transmission tower peeks open — his father had said the cinder of a man smoking his cigar. And now downtown the blinking neon of the largest sign on earth:

HANN

BROS

FURNITURE

I suppose you'll be leaving soon, she says. Youre a bird, arent you.

I'm going to university in three weeks.

I've got to finish school, she says, and then I'm taking a relaxation.

And what might that be.

Travel. In Greece I'll live with a German guy I met in Stephenville. There's a little island off Crete that he knows of and I've got circled on page thirty-four of my atlas. We write each other. He's twenty-three and he's a handsome Nazi.

I thought you were seeing a wrestler.

She turns her chin to her shoulder and looks at him.

So youre a spy, she says. A quiet spy. Well Hector has a hole in his heart, and I'm talking about his real heart.

I met a guy this spring, Gabriel says, in Trois-Rivières. I'm going to live with him in St John's. Alan knows a lot of French. He tries hard. I'm not competitive. Alan's French will improve and I'm going to live with him in residence. But I'm shy and I can't fail in front of others. Do you know French?

No.

Sometimes I'm afraid I know nothing.

It's hard to know anything.

But I can't even form an opinion.

There's nothing to be certain of these days. Except hunches. You can trust your guts. Do you think you could be gay?

I can see my mother thinking that. When I told her about Alan. She wouldnt let me buy a pea jacket. But no, I'm attracted to you.

Well that's very forward of you, Gabriel English.

Gabriel watches the blue darken. The details of the town slowly fading. Then the lights of Curling, Mount Moriah in behind. The bowl of lights of Corner Brook, first in lines as the roads brighten, then the white offices and yellow squares of houses. The smoke from the mill turns dark and then light against the dark.

They walk back down and catch a bus into Mount Moriah.

Nan Brennan says, Youre crazy to hitchhike to Montreal.

They could kill you and rape Doris and dump your bodies up north and you wouldnt be found for six months and you'd be just bone.

She takes Gabriel's wrist and says, If I was your age I'd snap you up. I'd crunch you in my teeth.

She holds his wrist hard.

Nan had been fishing in a flat boat made from plywood. She'd caught some healthy trout. There were geese in the reeds and a nest with one pale, abandoned egg.

They see a movie at the Majestic. On warm nights sitting on the grass by the *Western Star*, to watch the bright city bus turn, almost empty. Doris says they named the newspaper after a star that doesnt exist. It's called *Western Star* because Corner Brook is on the west coast of an island on the east coast of a continent which is called the western world. The grass is full of white flowers. They drink coffee at the mall and read first pages of books in Coles. They read aloud the first lines of new books. She suggests he cut the collars off his shirts and narrow the legs of his pants on her Nan's sewing machine.

Gabriel realizes, finally, that what his father had said of communism was not true. They would not all end up sleeping in the park. He had forgotten that he even still had that notion, but it comes to him and he rejects it.

He recognizes too that God probably does not exist in the way he had always envisioned him. There was mystery, to be sure, but not a single entity. The force in the world is a mist, though it still conveys a good message. The mist brings peace if you let it. It was like how some people can have strange children in their laps in four seconds. He understood too that Jesus didnt mean to imply that there was only one path. Each will find a route that's true.

They hitchhike to Port-aux-Basques, take the ferry to North Sydney, and get on the Trans-Canada for Montreal, ostensibly to see a retrospective of Picasso. Gabriel ends up driving for a man who wants to sleep through New Brunswick. He keeps the needle straining on a hundred and ten until the sun breaks onto the rear-view mirror and surprises him and Doris is reading aloud T.S. Eliot. Finally, the city with numerous grey, serious, multi-laned overpasses. They head for centre-ville. They sleep under a cement stoop and then one night beneath some scaffolding that is covered in silver tarpaulin beside a newly sandblasted bank. They wake with grit in their eyes and hair. They eat in diners and find a free map and they walk through Westmount and see Picasso's work at the museum and Gabriel thinks, I aimed to see Picasso and now I have done it. It was a new thought to will his life. They hitchhiked back the same route in twenty-three hours to the ferry and when they step down from a brand new school bus they'd met on the crossing, step down and see the pulp mill and Crow Hill and Blomidon mountains, they realize it had all taken less than eight days and nothing had happened here in the interim, although Doris did point out that the blueberries were not ripe here and that this was about to happen as they were ripe in Nova Scotia. This makes him wonder too if perhaps emotional states can ripen, maybe geography plays a role in your psyche and if he was going to McGill he might not feel so ignorant or if he went further south to an art college in Arizona, but there were no calendars for art colleges here.

There had been something in the curator's remarks, something about artists in Europe knowing if they were good enough and many when they were young — pianists especially — were told to become electricians, but Picasso was encouraged. The Germans in particular were very quick to stream their students and Gabriel wished there was someone German here to judge him.

He had slept with Doris for eight nights but they hadnt made love. This thing of love did not happen. Gabriel did not know the first thing and Doris knew he did not know and she wasnt about to educate him. He had heard the sound of a kiss when they were in the museum. Behind him a man and a woman had kissed and he had looked at Doris and it was as if they had kissed.

There was something she had said then about Christmas being winter and Easter was spring and they were ass-backward, that life and death should happen in reverse order and this made a difference to the symbolic weight of autumn.

But now they were back in Corner Brook and September was going to happen and he was going to buy a bus ticket for St John's and he knew already about the blueberries. On his bed there was a letter from student loans and one from Alan saying they'd been accepted at residence. Gabriel was going to Memorial to do something practical. That's what his parents had advised and he was still taking that as the caution of the world and good words to live by.

The Ground That Owns You

It was seven hours on the train. Elsie lay on the floor between us. Dark windows, a dim yellow light. We kept her on the blanket with Junior's sweater packed under her head to staunch the flow. We had never been this far east.

You boys should have put her out.

She moaned on every bump. At least Junior had given up on that. There was just us and Job Trask and Berta Jesso and Ellen Jesso in thick clothes with seven five-gallon buckets of partridgeberries and Sam Tobin who was also after grouse. The women had tough fingers. Job Trask shaking his head, kneeling.

That Al English's dog? You Al's? She been like that how long?

But he poured a cap of whisky on the wound, which made her tail knock. He tore off a strip of duct tape and wrapped it over her eye. From eight that night until three in the morning, sharing the clear whisky with his two women and Sam Tobin under the yellow strip light. They were all looking at Elsie as if to say they wouldnt have put her on the train. They would have finished her on the barrens and it's a misery to keep her like that. They were looking at us shameful. Beautiful dog, the blue belton. They hated to see something that good go to waste. The women sang to cover the moans and Job pressed his concertina. His brown fingers against the leather straps. Elsie's moans were like how large trees will creak standing still. They came from deep inside.

We pulled into Grand Falls at three a.m. and Job Trask woke up the vet. We slid Elsie and the blanket into the back of Job's green pickup. His red brake lights burning hot. Junior and I sat on the bright lids of the seven buckets of partridge-berries. Job and the two women rode in the cab, shoulders squeezed. Our shotgun barrels looking too long in the bed of the truck. And by four she was under an anaesthetic. Dr Ted Eriksson said he couldnt get all the pellet and he wasnt sure if there'd be any damage to the brain. There was no way he could save the eye.

I said to Junior, Vet wants to tear off a bit of our faces.

Elsie didnt stir until the sun was full off the trees. Dr Eriksson wrote out a pale blue bill and left us in the clinic, for it was Sunday. Junior was lighting smoke after smoke.

She looks bad, Gabe.

The vet had the socket sewn up and three other patches of black stitching on her forehead and jowl. It looked like she had a pile of ants mashed on her face. Elsie lay with her head on her front paws beside Junior with just her tail swishing. It was seventy-four dollars for the work on her face.

How you paying that off, Gabe?

Job Trask pulled up with Ellen and Berta Jesso. They came in with a plate of muffins and a thermos of tea. They took a look at Elsie. They checked her eye and said she's still smart.

You boys did fine. You leave that here when youre done.

And they piled back into the passenger side.

Those jackie tars, Gabe. Man, they live up there.

We waited in the clinic until noon, until Dad's red car with brown primer on the fender pulled up.

We had been sitting next to the rails. Elsie growling into the gravel. The creosote from the ties seeping into the ground. Junior had his topographical map of the Gaff bent over his knee. The railroad and the barren hills. Some of the transmission poles had been sawed down for fuel. All that's left is the tops hanging to the wires.

Gabe, I'm going to get some land off George's Road. Build a log house. There's some big spruce in there. I'm going to be a helicopter mechanic, there's money in that. I can work on the base in Stephenville. Or a bush pilot. Lou must be outfitting in Labrador. How much you figure land is in Labrador?

Uncle Lou a busher. Dad said to us when Lou went missing that at some time you have to return to the ground that owns you. But he hasnt come down yet. It's twelve years and he's still up there, hovering in the present. They havent found him, so up there he is and I figure he doesnt mind it one bit. When a plane flies by Junior will say, There goes Lou.

What do you think Dad's doing.

He's doing the kippers.

He's going to kill you.

She didnt heel.

Oh, so it's his fault.

Dad curing fish in the backyard. An elbow of aluminum pipe connecting the old bathroom sink cabinet to a barrel. Fresh herring, laid out in rows. Splits of wild cherry, smouldering. It's as good as hickory. The joke that he is smoking heroin.

Training Elsie with a partridge wing.

Fetch it, Else.

Elsie never pointing, just fetching.

You should shoot her, Gabe.

She's all right.

She's fucking bleeding to death.

You want me to shoot her with a number four?

I got a slug, Gabe.

We tried to keep her head up with Junior's sweater. The ground had no give. Just stone and caribou moss.

Why you got the slug?

I got three. You never know, Gabe.

He had them wrapped in a turn of newspaper.

If a caribou come out of that blaze, bang.

She got half her face tore off.

We didnt know the schedule. We took turns stroking her. Sometimes she wanted to paw at it and we had to keep her hind leg down. She bit me lightly each time I stopped her. Her jaws circled my wrist and she tugged but it hurt her face to do any more. She looked puzzled, as if she kept forgetting what was wrong. Those teeth around my wrist like a bracelet.

The wind rose because we were on the Gaff. That was good to keep off the blackflies. The burgundy bushes were turning blue and then the sun sank over Saucer Hill. Junior broke open his flask of Silk Tassel. We waited six hours for the train. We kept talking to her, good girl Elsie, come on Orelse. But we were getting tired of it. We were fed up with her moaning and the blood wouldnt coagulate. The barrens had turned to the colour of tattoos with grey patches of outcropping. There was no moon. It had trailed the sun all day by an hour.

It's three hours to Howley and there's no vet there. Steady Brook, four hours.

Junior said he couldnt if I said no, but if I wanted he could, with the slug, and then we could take the body with us any time. We had to be together on this. He said we could stay another day then and it wouldnt matter. We could put her in one of the fertilizer bags.

You going to paunch her too? Or just let her blow up.

Youre an asshole, Gabe.

And then we felt the vibration in the rails.

The sound's behind us.

Must be bouncing off the Gaff.

The beams of light arcing from the wrong direction. From the west with the wind.

Fuck.

Junior grabbed Elsie by the collar, to keep her there. How Dad would rub her nose in her mess if she did it inside.

We're going to fucking Grand Falls, Gabe.

Junior has a scar on his belly under the stomach. He's never trusted me since. I was cleaning trout in the lake in the dark. I had the flashlight trained on a spot of water. We had paddled up to Shoe Brook in the canoe and they were leaping around the old stump. A beaver slapped at the mouth of the brook. We fished until after dark. There was a whole moon they were jumping for. Casting the line over deep dimples. The caribou bug tied in the basement. The belief in what lies underneath. They were leaping against a curtain of bulrushes. On the way back the lights of cabins trickling over the surface, snipe tickling the shoreline. A loon was crying. The trout gave a thump on the floor of the canoe. The fibreglass drawing four inches so that the fish were under the waterline.

I like cleaning them. Dragging my thumbnail over the spine's zipper to scrape out the black. I was rinsing one and it gave a jerk. I had it gutted, but something in the muscles made it twist. With another, I was looking at the shameful load of orange roe. Then a movement behind me. A deep, low growl. I twisted quick, punching.

I was fucking joking boy.

June man June.

I had the knife in a good inch. He was wearing a cotton shirt.

Youre fucking manic.

The lake catches over as I freeze with the knife in my brother. We are ice-fishing on Finger Pond. The auger chipping through eight blue inches before the hollow plunge of water. Dad scooping out slush with a bare hand. We are careful with a slice of bacon in tinfoil. And when we have one trout caught we use its eyes, a piece of its face.

Elsie watching a lynx cross the frozen bog. She is biting off baubles of snow on her belly. Chewing the ice from between her webbed toes. We check out the lynx's trail. I wear my plywood snowshoes with holes punched through on my father's drill press. My father places my bare hand inside the paw print. He holds my wrist, guiding me in. My fingers touch the points of its claws.

The knife touches no organ.

I have never seen my father teach. He takes Junior and me to his school on the weekends. He rolls in the piano from the music room and plays while Junior and I prepare the fibreglass matting. The obscure drawings on two green chalkboards in my father's hand. The angles and degrees, the front, vertical and side views of gun racks. My father playing Chopin.

Holding the blueprints for the cabin, Dad says there is a map of the world larger than the world itself. It exists in a computer, an enlarged model of the earth's skin at a thousand to one. It meshes real photos from the space shuttle with a satellite geography of the earth. You can research any square inch of the earth's surface. There are people frozen in the act of crossing a street, he says. Sunbathing, fixing television antennas.

You can zoom in on spring chives punching through crisp brown leaves. The migration of land mammals. The carving out of rainforests. It took six days to collect all the pictures, but they make it appear as one day. As if you could nail down a day, he says. The whole earth in perpetual daylight. No dark side. Maybe we're in the map several times, Junior says.

We had cornered a covey of grouse on the bluff. Elsie pointing stiff. We were creeping up the sides. They were like moving rock, speckled granite, some of the oldest rock on earth. The wind flinching their feathers so you could see the down. The oldest thing I've ever touched, Junior says. Rock from the ocean floor.

We shot low just as they were lifting, before they had any speed, their wings up so the shot could hit the breast. Aiming a little ahead, into their future. That chuckle they give as they lift. And then it was Elsie filling up my sights.

She's not moving.

Elsie.

Fuck Gabe fuck.

She didnt heel.

You were aiming at the fucking ground.

I was at the grouse. You said low.

You fucking nailed her.

She was lying on her belly, her head straight out.

She's breathing.

Come on Elsie.

She was trying to crawl away from us.

What kind of name is Elsie. You can't go shouting Elsie over the barrens. You need a one-syllable name.

It was Elsie.

Orelse. That's what Junior called her.

You'd better do it Orelse.

At least it was her bad eye.

Elsie the runt. She had stumbled over the tall grass in Mr Dawe's backyard. Tripping towards her mother. Her brothers and sisters already taken.

It'll clear up in a few months.

I dont like her to have a rheumy eye.

I can knock down the price.

And there's no papers.

You can trust me, Al. The bitch is pure.

My father holding our chilled feet. We are hunting ducks in October. He tugs off our boots and damp socks. Junior says he's okay, but we're all a little numb. Dad blows in his hands and then cups my foot as if hiding it. He rubs the air in. He wiggles each toe, polishes my instep, the heel. Toes I had forgotten return to life. He is pressing the tingle of circulation back into them. It is his breath he is rubbing in.

As we lie in the tent my father says all lit moments are recorded in the distance of light. Every moment frozen in speed, beaming away from the earth. These moments exist in a solar wind. In the continuous flow of charged particles, moving farther from the reflected surface of earth. But things in the night, things hidden from windows, remain unlit, are unknown. Us lying here in this tent by the beaver dam. We're safe from history.

He says, slowly, that there is an island in Grand Lake called Glover Island. And Glover is the largest island on the island of Newfoundland. And on Glover there is a pond. And on that pond there is a smaller island. I want, he says, to paddle up Grand Lake and portage over Glover Island. Get to that pond and cross to the island and spend a night. He says there is only one other island in the world with a lake holding an island, and a pond on that island with an island in that pond, and that place is in Sumatra. And if you took a globe and put a finger on Newfoundland and another finger on Sumatra you'd see theyre pretty much on opposite sides of the earth.

The joists were numbered in white chalk. We had built the cabin in the industrial arts room. Taken it up in sections on the train. Junior had found a good station on the transistor. You could get everything up here. There were three grouse from the afternoon around the American Man cairn. Elsie had frozen on a patch of creeping juniper and I flushed them out while Junior nailed three with his over and under. The grouse were still brown even though it had snowed a little on the way up. They won't turn until October when it's good and white.

Our father was cleaning fish when we left him. We took the train and the dog in from Steady Brook. He was wearing the plastic apron I wore to bathe Elsie in the enamel sink. His chest covered in cod blood.

Before you shoot have a look in the distance. Know where your brother is.

The huge astonished heads of the cod, their innards hanging on to the skull like a root. Holding the filleting knife sharpened on the grinder. The light board for worms. The scales cutting the fish into two-pound bags. The deep freezer full of stiff wild meat in zip-loc bags.

My father told us he had visited Uncle Lou, when Lou lived in Florida. He'd heard the twin sonic booms as the space shuttle landed at the Cape and on a clear day you could see it rise.

He said Lou had been living illegally in Orlando, working for a garage at four American dollars an hour. This was before your aunt, he said. He came back for Aunt Brenda. But Lou had a woman in Orlando he thought about marrying in order to stay in the States. But she was a hard person to get along with, Dad said. She had views. They'd been living deep in Orlando, and yet he noticed something had been eating their tomato plants. Something wild. They were pulling into the driveway and caught a pair of eyes in the high beam. A possum. The middle of Orlando. They eat possum in Tennessee. My father took a shovel and followed the possum into the hedge. Gave it a pat between the eyes and threw the carcass in their landlord's backyard. It must have been thirty pounds of meat.

But the space shuttle. My father noticed it glinting in the daylight as it orbited. He figured it was dead over them, mapping the interior. He had some quotes for inland property, which was pretty cheap even compared to Newfoundland.

When Junior telephones I imagine my father's careful hands scooping water over his elbows, leaning in to rinse, the water trickling down the backs of his arms into the pink enamel sink. The elevator movement of his triceps, a soft muscle under the skin. The hair beginning at the elbow and ending at the bald knuckle of his wrist. My father cannot wear a watch. His body stops them. My father in a white undervest when the phone rings. It is six in the morning and he is about to start his Sunday. He has shaved, the smell of his beard burning on the hot motor. His glasses still folded against the mirror ledge. The only time I imagine his eyes closed. His small blue eyes like whitewater. Yes, he tells the operator. Youre where? Who shot her? Oh, you . . . fools.

It takes him five hours to drive the Trans-Canada. He packs a thermos of tea and a bag of dog food and stops at the Buchans turnoff for a cup of coffee. He sees three moose in the marsh by Pynn's Brook. He urinates in the ditch while log trucks roar past to the pulp mill. In Grand Falls he stops once for directions. Junior opens the clinic door. My father with the tips of his fingers in his front pockets, as if he is about to shove his hands in or take them out. It gives his shoulders a little rise. He holds his mouth firm. He looks at the empty muffin plate and the thermos. His dog.

Where were you and where were the grouse.

I point at the magazine rack about ten feet from Elsie.

And Elsie.

We map out the scene on the floor. Junior by the washroom, I am near the exit. Elsie where she is. My father standing alongside of me. You can follow the path of the shot, how the pattern caught the dog before it reached the grouse. You can tell the distance between my father and Junior and me.

You better put her in the back.

He takes the bill from my brother's hand and reads it. Then he folds it twice and pushes it into his jeans.

We sleep through most of the unfamiliar territory. Our father nudging us to show the turnoff for the mine and the road leading north to Gros Morne. We tell him of the Jessos and the muffins and he says what good people they are and how we should notice how they live in the land. He says the narrow-gauge railway will be gone soon and the Jessos will just hike in like theyve always done. Theyre selling the trains to Chile and the rails are going as scrap metal. The ties are used in flower beds. The entire railway lifted out of the land. The black line in the meat of a lobster tail.

A transport truck is tilted into the ditch. The trees and hills are much like the trees and hills we are used to. The Howley turnoff is the first thing I recognize and suddenly the land becomes warm.

Junior and I are trying to come up with the largest number in the world. A million, a billion, a zillion and four. Perhaps it's the bill. Junior says there's always a number larger. The windows are misted and Dad says there is one number larger than the rest. It is a special number that few know about and we should take care of it. And in the mist on the windshield he draws a sideways eight, like a racetrack. It is a number we have never seen before and my father names it.

A rise in the pavement means ten more minutes to Steady Brook. The town is built on a holm, which floods every few years. Elsie moaning at the quick drop in altitude. We pass the bend in the Humber where we first fly-cast from the boom. Our blue raincoats. The difference between salmon peal and trout marked on the boom with a charred stick from the fire. The forked tail, the speckles along the belly. But we forgot. There were so many trout, dozens, flicking them with a back cast into the long grass on the shore. Their bellies wriggling for water. We had them lined up on the boom. And the warden with his cream vest, waiting for our father who was fishing upstream. Each salmon peal, Mr English, could be a fine of two hundred dollars.

The water rushing to meet the paper mill at the Humber mouth, where deep grilse hold the ferocity of the sea in their muscles. Racing to the shallow force of river with the pulse of milt.

How many falls to make water pure?

Three, we say, together.

All three of us.

The Pallbearer's Gloves

Martin says, I've seen a man walk a wire forty feet up.

I've never seen that done live, I say.

He follows me, balanced, along the curb. Arms out, foot in front of foot.

And there was a half-alive gorilla, he says.

Half-alive?

Well, there was a man inside dressed up.

Martin says, You've got nice-from-behind legs.

I turn, What about the fronts?

Bony, he says. Bony as Daddy. And then he says, You know what? Daddy smells bad. But it's not him. It's what he spits up.

I lift him onto my shoulders. Martin says that Daddy had shown him where the hair was falling out. And new tufts like goose fur were underneath. He says the whole house had smelled bad and it stayed bad until after Daddy had been gone two days.

The bald man in grey pyjamas, with a strange new thinness in his hips. On his right side, the only way he could lie without the lung coughing. They had opened his ribs and left the lung in.

Bruce had said, It's me, Gabe.

I could recognize his voice.

You got a good view.

Oh terrific, he says. Trees. All day trees.

And it was trees. A sea of deep green with no deciduous for colour. It was fall and there would have been colour.

I brought you a photo.

Bruce studies the photo of Martin. He springs it between his fingers. Martin was doing things he hadnt seen. Dressed for kindergarten. There were the cherry and birch around their house, turning. Then his body gently shook. His large eyes closed tight.

He says, I'm sorry about this.

Bruce. It's okay.

I take his hand. I have never taken his hand. I have, but we were very young, crossing a street.

I say, You must be terrified.

No. Not terrified. It's terrible.

I hold the hand tightly. There is a laxness in the tone of the muscles. He lifts himself to spit in a plastic bucket, and I see the staples on his chest. The pyjamas from Mom. His spit smells of sharp chemicals, a clear liquid that had flowed into his arm a week before. They use this stuff, he'd said, grinning, in chemical warfare.

I ask if there's anything I can do. Anything.

He says, Helen doesnt visit enough.

Junior arrives from Florida. He brings his girlfriend, Carol. I greet them at the airport.

Hiya Gabe, she says. Wow, Junior, your family all this tall?

She hugs me hard. She seems proud of me. As if Junior had something to do with how I turned out, which is probably true.

We wait for their luggage. And stretched out on the carousel is a six-foot-tall stuffed Sylvester. For Martin.

Junior: Hey, they broke his neck.

Carol: His neck is all wonky.

On the way into town Junior holds Sylvester's neck and turns the head out the window. He says, Look, Sylvester, guardrails. *In* the city. Man, we're back in the sticks.

I say, You want to go to Signal Hill?

No, Gabe. Straight to your place. No, stop in to Butcher's.

I drive down to Water Street. Butcher's is a strip club that Junior used to work in. Carol says, I'm staying for one drink.

The bouncer takes Junior's hand in an arm-wrestling gesture and Junior says, Theyre with me. In a booth Carol leans over her drink and, while Junior is talking to the bouncer, she says, We're married. She says this as if it's something she was not supposed to reveal.

She says, Junior wanted to stay down there and apply for a green card. So I said, Honey, let's get married. And we got married. But he doesnt want you all to know because, he says, we married for the wrong reason. But we love each other now, dont we, honeybun?

She grabs him around the waist and he leans reluctantly.

Junior: Mom'll be really mad if she finds out.

What do you mean if.

He nods a find-the-right-moment nod.

The bouncer gives Junior a playful punch on the biceps.

Junior: We were split up on the plane, Gabe, so I offered this guy, business guy, sitting next to me, twenty dollars American if he'll switch seats with my wife. Guy says, No need for that.

The next day I take them to the hospital. We bring a pineapple. I realize too late that I havent prepared Junior well enough. I havent, until that moment, noticed the disintegration of Bruce. Junior sinks a little at the knees.

Hi, bro.

June.

I cut the top and heel off the pineapple, then slice it vertically like a pie. Carol introduces herself. I hand round wedges of pineapple. Bruce: This is the way to eat pinochle.

Junior: You growing sideburns?

Bruce: Only hair I got.

I have told Junior to talk, to entertain. He goes: I gave Carol a few driving lessons, Bruce. She said Junior, one hand on the wheel. I'm used to driving with my knees, see. Fifteen years of driving with my knees. But she wants one hand. This is Disneyland, not Newfoundland. And then she doesnt like how I'm passing. I tell her, You need momentum, Carol. You can pass anything if you got momentum. You flow through traffic. But she says, Youre getting too close. So I slow down. Then there's two-lane passing. And she says okay. And I look at her. I had momentum back there, but now I got no momentum. You want me to build another cylinder on the head of your block? And then, on a curve, I take this Porsche. For a joke. Porsche doesnt like that. Comes right back on a straight-away, zipping. And I say Oh yeah, youre fast, buddy. You can take a little Tercel on a hill with my wife and the dog in the back and a fifty-pound bag of blue potatoes over my shoulder. Oh yeah youre speedy.

Bruce: Your wife.

Look, that piece of information.

Junior raises a finger to his lips. We have been withholding information all our lives.

You got a good place down there?

Oh yeah, Bruce, nice. There's cockroaches with wings. I let the reptiles go, theyre too hard to hit with a towel — though I've killed a few with my blow gun. Nailed them to the ceiling, but Carol doesnt like that, do you Carol. Junior pauses. And youre going to a good place, Bruce.

What's that.

Youre going somewhere good.

Another pause.

You mean heaven.

Yeah, heaven.

I'm not going to heaven.

Yes, Bruce.

I'm going there, but not now.

He clasps a hand around the bone in his thigh. He says: Gabe thinks I'm going to live a long time.

You are, I say.

Junior rubs the seam at the side of his jeans. He says, Does Helen have a lot of wood? I'm gonna get her a massive turkey for Christmas. Is the house well insulated? You can take off one of the outlets to check.

Bruce closes his eyes and smiles. Think I can have a piece of that turkey?

And then Helen and Martin arrive, Martin with no shirt on. Helen calm. She hasnt seen Junior in, what, five years? Bruce, quickly: It's been three. We were all together before Junior left.

In the hallway Junior says, That's it, Gabe. I'm quitting smoking.

Junior and Carol fly to Corner Brook to be with Mom. And then they drive in together in Junior's old Cordoba. He took it off blocks and drained the cylinders of oil. Junior: We were in a gas station, Gabe. Mom was looking in the coolers, she doesnt want a coffee. Orange crush, she says. Ooh, cream soda. *Red* cream soda. So I take her, tender like, by the shoulder and say, Mom. You dont get out much, do you.

Junior tells her Bruce is on the way out. His head has shrunk, his eyes are goggly and he's got no legs. Mom is clenching her ears. It's as if the muscles in her temples are seized shut.

Bruce the eldest, but still a young man, just forty-two. He still has a quick look in his eyes. I say, Do little exercises. Lift your legs, Bruce. Youve got to get your strength.

But I cough, Gabe. It saps me.

I've been visiting every day. I sit in the blue chair and read from my journal, from stories I'm writing. He asks if I'm interested in him and I say of course. That it's all down, everything. He says he's keeping a diary. He's writing down his life for Martin.

When they move him to the palliative care unit his spirit improves.

You can open the window here, he says.

And the Waterford River. There's houses and traffic. With the window open the city is with him in the room.

In the hallway is a large stained glass, he says. And the nurses coddle you. They bring poached eggs in ceramic cups.

It's here that his family has come for the last time.

Helen had this plan. To have Bruce home for an afternoon. So he could admire the outdoors through his windows. She'd rent a car. But Junior doubted it.

It would probably kill him.

But he would have that afternoon.

I know that's all he wanted. One afternoon in the light of his living room. A little medieval music on the stereo, the soft juniper. Martin coming home from kindergarten with his recess box and the two zip-loc baggies. His knapsack with gym sneakers and a colouring book. The sneakers too small so he wears thin socks. A boiled egg with toast cut into soldiers. The couch and the cat and a strip of the bathroom if you turn your head. The stained deck with some split birch for the woodstove.

Junior: Bruce thinks he's going to get better.

What else can he think.

He can be realistic.

You can't be realistic. Death isnt realistic.

We drive to Helen's. Over the moonscape of rock near Avondale. The sun punches through and lights up a knoll here, a valley there. The burgundy blueberry bushes, small bowls of grey ponds. If I were to make a film, I'd have a scene here.

At Helen's. I hear Mom say about a book, If I was interested in the subject I would have been very impressed.

We walk around the pond. Junior notices a thin film of ice has just caught over. I ask him why water sinks as it gets colder, but rises before freezing. He says there is no good reason for it. It's one of the reasons he believes there is a God.

Looking at the canoe in the dark. Martin: It looks blue but I know it's green.

Junior: If it's blue it's blue.

Junior's wife cuts Martin's hair. And then Helen's. And then Mom and me. I've got a weight line in back. Carol does the Newfoundland accent and Helen does the Florida. Martin says, Carol's favourite saying is, Dont you just hate that?

Helen is shaking a cast iron pan full of hot Italian sausages and onion. Carol cuts up three tomatoes theyve brought from Mom's garden. Garlic and crushed chili. The sausages spit and cry. I put on water for pasta. Martin watches me lay plates in the oven to warm.

Mommy, he's cooking the plates.

Carol says, Everything with meat in it is really different between here and down there.

Junior: Fat. Fat content. Down there ham is laced with fat.

Helen says she's glad theyve come now. There's no need, she says, for you to visit after.

Mom: It's all bullshit anyway, what they'd be saying at his funeral. Because it's not the truth, is it.

Junior: I'm coming when he dies. I'm coming both times.

Junior and I paddle to the island. We take it slow to slice the ice. I have to spot for rocks. It's Bruce's canoe. The ice splits like torn paper. Junior takes a beer that he balances on the floor of the canoe. Bruce, he says, wouldnt cut the trees here because he wanted to look at them.

He's a man of beauty.

He says, What do you think of Carol?

She's great.

She's a little fat, dont you think.

I think she looks great.

And I dont like how she treats me in front of Mom.

Junior. She's funny and she's strong.

She's got two kids in Tampa, did you know?

I hadnt heard that.

He says, We've been fighting. She'll go back now and strip the apartment down and move back to her mother. I know it.

I hear him glug the beer and toss the bottle. It smashes the ice and bobs.

I need a challenge, he says. I got a Honda CRX. So small I wouldnt survive in it. I killed a vulture with a .357 Magnum. Big guy. Fucking around with my pork chops. He was trying to swoop down on them. One shot, poacher's rule. If you shoot twice, warden can tell, he can echo-locate you.

When I hear this, it sounds like He can electrocute you.

I'll come home for three weeks, Gabe. In November. The van is my safety net. If I fall I got the van.

On the paddle back he shows me the J stroke.

Have you told Mom yet?

No, Gabe. I was gonna tell her and then she whispered to me — she'd been eyeing Carol — she said no matter where I am she'd come to my wedding.

Junior leans back against the gunwales and stares at the sky. Out here you get the stars. He says, I live between two bodies of water, Gabe. You got to come down. Gulf of Mexico and the North Atlantic.

The North Atlantic?

Yeah, Gabe. Atlantic is still the north, even in Florida. I drive east after work, in the dark, and there's lightning. And in behind the lightning there's an orange atmosphere. From the sun. The sun has sunk but the light's still there, banking off the clouds, in the dark. That's the best time of day, driving home in that left-over light.

Helen is making tea. Junior is finishing a box of beer and eating out the fridge shelf by shelf. He wants a cigarette terribly. My mother has her legs up on the couch. She is reading scripture. Martin in bed.

Helen says she had woken to Bruce struggling. He couldnt get enough air. The ambulance service coating the tops of trees with orange light. And now it's been sixty-one days. Helen says she knows. That some people find her behaviour callous: They can't believe how I'm treating Bruce. Your husband. Bring him home, they say. They visit and wait for their cup of tea and cake. Their sandwich and a dill pickle. They sit right where you are and demand service. And I have to work and take care of Martin and drive into town and visit Bruce and boil a kettle for them while they sympathize and tell me what a loving wife would do, what they would do for poor Bruce. Well, shag them.

Mom looks up from Romans. She says, The trouble is you have no past. This kind of thing you expect to happen in your sixties. And by then youve stuck by the person. You nurse them through anything because of that past. Bruce got sick too early.

Youre saying I'd do more if I was seventy.

A sudden hatred overtakes us. Helen: And I suppose you'll be writing all this down, she says. Colder than a witch's tit.

I have never heard her use this tone.

Mom: You could see how besotted Bruce was. When Helen said she'd marry him. He called me once and I said, Well, Bruce, youve got yourself a woman there. I hope there won't be any complaints. And he said, No, Mom I won't complain. That was six years ago. And when I saw him at the hospital and asked how he was he said, quietly, I've got no complaints. I know he was thinking about that. He never forgets those things.

Helen, relenting: You must write about the things that you love.

Junior's eyebrows go up and he nods to me. It's midnight now and I follow him outside. At the wood pile: Gabe, zip zip?

Junior holds Helen's chainsaw.

Quit it.

Got to, Gabe.

You'll wake Martin.

You dont want to help your sister-in-law?

You dont know what I do.

I know you dont zip wood.

I dont do a lot of things.

You dont paint her house.

I'm scared of heights.

Just a little, Gabe. Hold the logs. Just stack for me.

Sorry.

Afraid of wood in general?

I'm not interested in wood.

Keeps you warm. Keeps the snow off you. Wood's pretty interested in you.

I like dealing with it in my own time.

You like to get around to it.

I like taking my time.

Sort of saunter up to it.

I dont like the pace you set.

You dont like to get it done quick.

I like to enjoy my moment with the wood.

Yeah, Gabe, I can see that's your whole problem. You like to enjoy a moment with the wood. A little station break with your meal ticket. Gabe, you got to do things quick. Get in, get out. Dont fuck around in there. Speedy, man. Points are dirty.

Junior starts scraping at the plug with a screwdriver.

I say, The moment is all we have.

Youve got the future. The whole fucking works in front of you.

Me: I thought you were a moment-by-moment kind of man.

Moments yeah moments. But I got a plan, Gabe. I got the future. Right here.

Junior taps his temple with the screwdriver.

I tell him I have a hard time believing it. There's no future for Bruce.

Oh but that's unfair. That's unusual. He's what you'd call a worst-case scenario.

I'd call him my brother. Dying.

Oh so he's dying now.

I never said he wasnt.

Funny, thought I heard it.

All I ever said was, he looks to me like he's getting better. That he's a young man. He's putting on weight.

That's water, Gabe. He's bloated. He's a dead man.

Well, perhaps it's not the best thing to tell that to his face.

Junior lays the chainsaw on the woodhorse.

You saying I told him that.

You told him he's going to heaven.

I said, Youre going to a good place. I did not say, Bruce youre a dead man.

I get the phone call in the small hours. It's still dark.

This is Joan at the palliative care unit? I'm afraid Bruce's taken a turn.

I drive under a full moon, eating an apple. The quiet, empty, blue city. I clomp down the dark corridor in heavy boots on the red tiles. I didnt realize how loud the boots were. Joan intercepts me. She says you just missed him.

In the hot room he is lying on his back. The first time I've seen him on his back in months. Just a small yellow lamp on. His feet and knee caps poking up the white sheet. His eyes are open. His head hot and I can hear breathing, except it's from the man across the hall.

I help Joan peel the art off the walls and we drape the art over his legs because there is nowhere else to lay it. I sit with him until Helen comes.

Helen: What do you think.

Me: Put the white shirt on him. And the tie.

Helen: He never wore ties.

He wore slacks with sneakers.

He's not going to have any shoes. And he never wore underwear.

Helen, youve got to have him in underwear.

He doesnt have any. He had raggy old pairs. I think he expected me to get him some and I never did.

Let me get the underwear.

Helen is drinking brandy from a mason jar as Ed Chafe plays guitar with his left foot resting on his right. Bruce is laid out in his white Edwardian shirt. Junior talking to Harold Drover about polar bears: the only animal that will stalk us as if we're just another animal, like seals. Harold: Yams are the only food you can live on. Martin asks why guests get fed first. Mom: they wouldnt come if they were fed last.

I am a pallbearer along with Arnold Hicks and Helen's two brothers and Mike Pierce and Harold Drover. Junior was asked, but he said he was too tall to carry it. We wear white cotton gloves. Martin wants a pair. I say, I'll give you mine when we're done.

I need a lift and the hearse driver says I can go with him. So it's me and Bruce and the driver in the hearse, cruising to Conception Harbour. Bruce in the box between us. A sign: USE APPROVED DEEP FAT FRYERS. The sky low and dark and sad. There is no wind and the sea is some calm, the driver says. Hasnt seen it so flat in ages. All the colours of the woods thrown into the harbour.

I guess you do this a lot, I say.

Oh yes, he says. I know this road well.

There is a shoe streak of dog shit on the church steps, and

not much room to get through. The hushed, full church. I am surprised there are people. Helen drapes a sheet over the coffin. Junior holds Martin as she does this. Martin a little bored, but he stays quiet. Then he walks proudly around the pews to his friends. There is a young minister, the pews are full. I'm surprised by the numbers and it makes me feel some kind of hope. Hope had gained ground on desolation.

We carry the coffin out of the church as the pews sing How Great Thou Art and I can hear Mike Pierce sobbing behind me at that surge of music — and the poet Andy Meades, I see his hand with a big black stone ring. Andy takes my gloved hand and holds it as we walk down the aisle with the coffin and that song, which is a powerful, positive song, a strong song with all those voices in it. We carry him out to the car and drive to the cemetery, which overlooks the blurred hills of Avondale. There is a brown horse in a field and the gravediggers rest beside a backhoe and a truck. The pallbearers stand around the grave and Helen places a dry shaft of golden wheat on the coffin. The head undertaker lowers the coffin on a hydraulic system operated by his shoe. I watch the pallbearers tug off their gloves and lay them on the casket as it sinks. I do the same. When the lid is flush with the surface they stop and cover it with green felt.

I say to Helen, No one takes pictures at a funeral. She says she'd noticed that and wished someone had. Of Martin playing around the new tombstones and of the pallbearers' gloves. Andy Meades says he thought about taking a camera but didnt know if it was proper. Junior mentions the spectacle of past funerals, of horses with black plumes. The sky had cleared and it's warm and sunny. Bruce's given us a good day, our mother says, smiling.

We walk out to Helen's brother's house. Patrick. We eat white triangles of sandwiches. Junior leans over to check the legs of a black chair. He says, A Windsor chair. You know how old this is, Gabe? It used to be green. It would have been used on a porch. It was painted black when Queen Victoria died. There are no squares, he says, on a good chair.

When we leave, Patrick says: Now dont be a stranger — and dont be a fixture either.

Martin puts his legs over my ribs. I can feel his short breaths. The lightness of him balanced on me.

Youre Daddy.

I'm not Daddy.

Pretend youre Daddy.

What would Daddy do.

He would snuggle right in.

I take Martin one night a week. We have supper then read and it's bedtime. The first time he threw up and I asked him about it. He was embarrassed. He'd tried to cover the vomit in the sheet. He'd made a little pocket of it and tucked it under the pillow. He said he'd woken up and didnt know where he was. He didnt recognize anything and that had scared him. And he wasnt that fond of supper and up it came. I said, You want to get in with me? and he said, Of course.

Youre my favourite uncle.

And youre my favourite nephew.

He kicks. I'm your only nephew.

He asks where Daddy is now. I say he's in God's book. Martin says, Is he in heaven. Is he with Mrs Tuft and her knitting socks for all the angels? I say he's in God's book and when God remembers everyone you'll see him again.

We watch a videotape that I took with Bruce on the ice of the pond. The audio was broken on the camera so it's just pictures. Bruce and Helen walk out on the ice, about halfway out, their backs slightly bent, testing its strength. They do an impromptu dance. Bruce is wearing a navy Russian coat and a fur hat. His beard. And he starts the dance. Or perhaps the camera prompts it. Or maybe it's Martin urging them. But they waltz over the pond with Martin chasing, falling, and you can almost hear Martin's screams. The next frame jerks to black and then it's me and Bruce on the ice. We stand looking at each other, our feet, still. Our breath in steady blue puffs. Martin, you can tell, is telling us to dance. But we box. We shadow-box over the ice, just like when we were kids, feinting. And Helen loses interest in us as she finds a juniper bare of needles covered in silver thaw. You can see the camera's indecision and then choice. The camera pans off the boxers to study that dormant, glittering juniper. And you know that Martin is somewhere below, some place screaming for the men to dance, grabbing at their bare hands.

Archibald the Arctic

Early on New Year's Day my mother woke me to say, calmly, that two police officers were at the door. She said this in the same way she'd say there's a fried egg sandwich in the oven. I was seventeen, home for Christmas, staying in Junior's room, in his bed in fact. I had been out with Geoff Doyle and Skizicks the night before, we ended up on Crow Hill throwing our empties down on the tracks, enjoying the wet distant crumple they made, waiting for the fireworks to sputter into the cold dark air. I remember Skizicks, who is a year older and knew we were virgins, saying he'd screwed Heidi Miller against the wall in behind Tim Horton's. Over the course of two long minutes we counted the reports of eleven shotguns, sounding small, disorganized and lonely.

I walked to the porch in my cold jeans, barefoot. I was hungry and my head hurt. I worked my mouth. The police officers were still outside. I opened the screen door. The white metal handle was frosty. Snow was drifting lightly onto their new fur hats, their epaulets, sliding off the waxed cruiser which hummed quietly in behind my father's car. There were no lights flashing. The driveway needed to be shovelled. Doyle would be up in his window, if he was up. The officers were facing each other, conversing. Snowflakes tangled in their eyelashes. Their footprints were the first to our door in the new year. They looked fit and very awake.

Are you Gabriel English?

Yes.

We have a warrant for your arrest, son.

I knew there was something you could say here. I searched for the proper wording.

Can I ask what the charge is?

We'll discuss that at the station.

Am I under arrest?

This is what my father had taught us. When the law wants you, ask if youre under arrest. I was glad I could remember it.

We'd prefer to formally charge you down at the station, son, after we've cleared a few things up.

My father, who had been in the bathroom shaving, came to the door. He was still in his undervest, mopping his neck and chin with a white towel. He wasnt wearing his glasses, which gave him a relaxed look. He said, Would it be all right, fellas, if the boy had some breakfast? I'll bring him down right after.

The way he dried himself with the towel showed off his massive, pale biceps, his thick wrists. The thickness was well earned. There was a beat and then the older officer said that would be fine. He decided to look at my father for a moment and then they turned and made new footprints back to the cruiser.

My father turned to me and said, Well what a way to start the new year. He said this in a way that reassured me. He knew already that I hadnt done anything, that I wasnt capable of doing a bad thing. He was confident about this, all he knew about me was good things. I was the good son. His impression reinforced a faith in my own innocence. It made me realize what must have happened and suddenly I got upset.

It's Junior, isnt it, he said.

I suspect it's Junior, Dad.

And why do you suspect him.

He knew that I must be in league with Junior, had information that we'd kept from him. Over breakfast I told him what I knew. He listened as if, while the particulars of the event were new to him, they fit into the larger maze which was the interlaced lives of his sons. He said, Theyre going to begin with a presumption. That youve been driving. And you havent. Be flat out with that and the rest hold to your chin. He said, People in charge like to figure things out. They dont appreciate confessions.

We drove to the police station, which was a bunker below the Sir Richard Squires building. The building housed the first elevator in Newfoundland.

I liked the Up and Down arrows by the elevator buttons.

That was my earliest appreciation of technology's ability to appear prescient. I thought it was a considerate touch by the makers. The elevator was the avenue to Corner Brook's public library, which my father had introduced to me before I could read. I would pick up books Junior had chosen, like *Archibald the Arctic* and stare at the riddle of print. Junior loved the northern explorers — of men eating their dogs, and then each other.

The lobby was glass on three sides, with nine storeys of brick pressing down on it. My father took me to the sixth floor once, to a government office where he had some tax business. I could see the Bowater mill, the neck of the bay twisting around the town of Curling, the swans (the whitest things in town) drifting below in the reservoir which cooled the mill's furnaces, the secondary schools on the landscaped hill to the east. I was uneasy in the building. I was convinced the glass footing would topple. I worried for the commissionaire stationed at his desk by the fountain.

The fountain stood in the centre of the lobby behind an iron railing. It drizzled water over its scalloped and flared glass edges. A boy was carefully tossing a penny in. The fountain was a silent, enormous presence, a wordless example of grander things one could value and live for. I loved the fountain even when no one and nothing told me it was worthy of love.

My father leaned against the rail. He said if he had guts, he'd sell everything and help the poor in Calcutta. That was his base belief about what was right. His weakness drove him to self-interest, to preserving family and constantly bettering our material position. He could appreciate decorative flourishes, but never allowed himself to get carried away.

My mother would say I have these thoughts because we emigrated from England. My mother has given a lot of time to such considerations. She cultivates hindsight, and researches the repercussions of certain acts. Perhaps if I had grown up where I was born, had not felt strange in my own skin, I wouldnt be so sensitive in the world. In the house I spoke with an English accent, outside I pronounced words the way Doyle and Skizicks said them. I said brakfest, chimley, sove you a seat. I was aware of the boundary between blood bond and friends, between house and world. Junior was different. He managed to be pure Newfoundlander.

My father and I walked down to the police station and I began my brief story of never having driven a Japanese car in Alberta and the officer nodded as if he knew the truth of the matter only too well, that my arrest was a technicality, that a million brothers a month pretend to be younger brothers and he was going to add this latest infraction to the pile. I was free to go.

The station, below the library, was a place I had been to only once before, when Doyle and Skizicks and I were accused of breaking a window. We were kicking stones down Valley Road and a neighbour's window crashed in. We ran. We ran home. Junior said, When youre in trouble, where do you run?

Home.

No, Gabe, always run away from home.

I found the station small and casual. It didnt look hard to break out of. There were three cells in the back that I could only hear.

I never spoke to Junior about this arrest. He had left to go back to Alberta on Boxing Day. He was plugging dynamite holes in Fort McMurray.

My father has cried twice — once when a German shepherd we had ran from his knee and was crushed by a snow plough, the other when Junior left to work in the tar sands. It doesnt hurt me to think of him crying for Junior and not for my departure, or even crying for a dog we rescued from the pound, a thin, shivering creature who knew who to thank for fattening him up. He became too fierce in protecting us. Crying is an irrational act and should never be resented. I know Junior's life is a riskier thing. I know that my parents trust my good sense (I am named executor of their wills). There will be greater love attached to wilder men.

Before Christmas I went out with Junior to a cabin belonging to one of the Brads. Junior knew three men named Brad, and my mother had begun to disbelieve him. That they had other names. She would answer the phone and say, No, he's off somewhere with one of the Brads. As if that was a joke and she wasnt to be fooled. But I believe they were all called Brad. I think perhaps naming someone Brad is not a good idea.

Brad picked us up in his black and gold Trans Am and tried

his best to charm our mother who appreciated the gesture but still kept her opinion. I sat in the back and we detoured down Mountbatten Road. We stopped at a house with blue aluminum siding. Brad honked his horn and a screen door opened with two women waving and smiling and pointing a finger to indicate one moment. Brad popped the trunk from inside and waited.

Who are they.

Our wool blankets.

The girls climbed in the back and I remembered Linda from a party Junior had at the house. She had come into my bedroom, sat on the floor with a beer, and told me how she loved Junior to bits.

They nudged me with their hips to get their seat belts on. I was in the middle. Then Linda smiled: Youre gonna be our chaperon, Gabe. Danielle leaned forward and pulled on Brad's hair and kissed him on the ear and I could see the perfect contour of her breast.

Brad Pynn had a cabin up in Pynn's Brook. Junior liked to go snowmobiling and drinking up there over the holidays. He'd flown into town, gotten his presents giftwrapped by Linda at the hardware store he used to work at, and invited her to Brad's.

Brad and Junior had a plan to rob the small bank above Co-op grocery on Main Street. I dont mind revealing this because, to my knowledge, they never pulled the heist and now, I believe, the bank is closed. It was a small bank, used by members of the Co-op. It was less formal than other banks.

There were just desks, rather than counters with glass. You could walk right into the safe if you were quick. Junior was convinced you could pull off that job. The only problem was, everyone knew him. And if you did it with someone like a Brad Pynn, you could never be sure if he'd blow too much money one night, or brag, or betray you.

This bank scheme was something that always came up after a few beers, or during a vial of oil and a sewing needle, which Junior had out in the front seat, spreading the green oil over a cigarette paper on his knee. The joint was passed and I had to take it from Danielle, smoke, and hand it to Linda. Danielle kept pressing my knee saying, Look at that, if she saw a cute house, or a crow on the melted road that refused to lift. She'd press my knee then slide her hand a little up my thigh, as though she'd forgotten it was my thigh. Linda put her arm along the back window to make more shoulder room. They were quite relaxed.

Junior had a sawed-off shotgun between his legs which I watched him load with a red number four shell. He asked Brad to roll down his window. Cold air pummelled into the car. He clicked the chamber closed. He lifted the barrel up to Brad's windowsill, pushed off the safety, stared back at us and said, Watch this.

He saw Danielle's hand on my thigh and Linda's arm around my neck and paused.

There were three black objects ahead standing in the snow on Brad's side of the highway. Brad kept the speedometer at the limit. Junior didnt aim, just pointed at the grade and estimated the distance. He fired and the crows flew up alertly. Brad swerved.

Jesus, June.

He slipped off the road, hit bare ice, fishtailed, adjusted for the swing, pumped the brakes a little, and straightened up. The blast echoed inside the car. Junior was laughing until he saw that Linda and Danielle were horrified. We all saw, through a thin veil of trees, a line of cabins. People.

Oh, honey. Sorry about that.

Linda clenched her jaw and stared out her window. Her arms crossed and flexed.

Brad owned a Gold Wing which he parked and chained into the cabin over winter, and this bike he straddled and drank beer from and turned on the stereo embedded in the ruby fibreglass windjammer and would have started it up if Junior hadnt, at Brad's request, drained the cylinders and cleaned his valves and left the engine to hibernate in drenched oil.

Brad and Junior took the purple Arctic Cat for a bomb down the lake to ice-fish and to hunt with the sawed-off. They carried a small auger and they had slugs in case of a moose. The girls and I played Scrabble and drank rum mixed with Tang crystals. I missed touching their arms and hips. They were about twenty, both attending the Career Academy and slowly becoming disappointed. But that winter they were still bright, talkative Newfoundland women who wore friendship rings and small twinkling earrings and could imagine ways to have fun and succeed. They'd spent summers working in the fish plant in Curling and winters wearing white skates on ponds like Little Rapids. I could tell they enjoyed me and while each on her own might have been bored with my company, together they shared a glee in flirting, in egging me on. In their eyes I was a man in the making, and I accepted this. Women like a confidence no matter what the confidence is.

Linda said, Youre going to be something, arent you. Youre like your brother, but youre smarter and gentle.

Ah, Linda he's shy, boy.

And Danielle put her arm around my neck and felt my ear. Her collarbone lifted a white bra strap. Shy? Why you got nothing to be shy about.

She slipped her hand down to my waist.

Have you ever done the dirty? she said.

I didnt have to answer and they laughed and loved the fact that now they were getting into this.

You know something me and Linda have wanted to do?

Linda felt my crotch. She put a hand in my jeans pocket.

Wow. Danielle. Guess what he's not wearing.

Go way.

Danielle slipped her hand in my other pocket. This pocket had the lining torn and her warm, probing hand clasped directly and gently.

Oh, Linda, we've got a fine young man on our hands.

A growing boy.

Linda unbuttoned my jeans. I shifted in my chair and prayed that the skidoo would be loud. I tried to recall the sound it made as it buzzed up the lake. But as it was, even if

Brad and Junior came in the door, nothing could be seen above the table. Nothing except an astonished boy and two eager, laughing women leaning in to him.

Last fall Junior hit a moose. This was six days after the mandatory seat belt law had been established, and it was this law which had saved his life. Dad and I found him unconscious, pinned behind the wheel of his orange-and-chrome VW Bug. Eight hundred pounds of moose had rolled over the hood, crumpled the windshield, bent the doorframes and lay bleeding in his lap. The ambulance service had to wait for the jaws of life to free him. He'd loved the Bug, it had lived its previous life in salt-free Florida. Investigators measured skid marks, the animal was towed off with two canvas cables, its injuries charted, witnesses signed statements and it was declared that Junior had been driving with abandon under severe winter conditions.

He bought a Rabbit then, and two weeks later he rammed into the back of an eighteen-wheeler; the Rabbit was dragged four hundred metres before the semi braked. The trucker was furious, he hadnt even seen Junior, he was that far up his ass. Up your wind tunnel, Junior said, looking for an opportunity to pass. The trucker wanted to smack him. He would have if my father hadnt stretched his big hands in an obvious way.

Junior began giving up on a Datsun, an old, whipped car. He was motoring around town, scouting for other drivers' infractions. Someone running a red light. If he saw anything, he drove into it. He was making money, he said, from other people's insurance.

When the Datsun had built up a nest egg he asked if I wanted to go for a ride. This was after supper, in early December. He'd decided, he said, to retire the vehicle. The insurance company had declared it a liability and he had to write it off before the calendar year.

We drove to the empty, carefully ploughed parking lot behind the school my father taught at. The street lamps were just flickering on. It was terminally ill, Junior said, and we had to put it out of its misery.

He revved up the motor, spun on the slightly icy pavement, and swaggered the car towards a ploughed mound of snow at the edge of the lot.

Hold on, Gabe.

The headlights lurched, grew in concentration against the bank as we accelerated and approached. The car exploded into compact snow, driving in a few feet, snow smacking against the windshield, the hill absorbed our blow. The motor muffled, hummed, still ran happily. If it had a tail it would be wagging.

Junior shifted into reverse, hit the wipers, spun wide, and galloped for the opposite end of the lot, dipsy doodling around a street-light pole on the way, swinging on the ice and slamming sideways into the far bank of snow.

I had to get out and push this time. The exhaust was clogged with snow. I watched as Junior aimed for a sturdier bank pressed against the school. The car whined horribly. There was no give in the snow. The seat belt cut against his chest as he came up hard on a hidden concrete post. A crease formed in the hood of the car, the grill burst open and jets of water spouted up, dousing the windshield and melting then freezing the snow on the hood. The motor kept running as if nothing had happened. I ran to him.

Can't kill a fucking Datsun, man.

Junior got out to reconsider his approach. I reminded him that if he went through with this demolition we'd have to walk home. He popped the hood (it opened at the windshield) and cranked up the heat to transfer valuable degrees over from the engine. Then he said come look at this.

We stood on the front bumper and stared into the dark classroom. On the board were the yellow chalk drawings our father made of various projects: tables, lamps, chairs. There were angles and choice of wood screw and the correct use of a plane and a clamp. The work tables were cleared, the tools all hanging in their racks, the cement floor swept with sawdust and water. Everything in order.

We drove home with the broken radiator, my eyes fixed to the temperature gauge, which hovered past the orange bar.

It was then Junior asked me for a favour. We were parked, the lights shut off, the engine ticking to the cold. He said his insurance was sky-high. What we'd do, he said, is insure his next car in my name and he'd be a second driver. It would save him a hell of a lot of cash.

At the time I wasnt driving anything and when youre not using something, it's hard to feel the importance of giving it away. There was a mature air about Junior needing my help in the adult world. But a warning hunch spread through my body. I knew there would be repercussions, though I could not articulate them. It all seemed reasonable, he just needed to borrow my driver's licence for an hour.

It wasnt just the insurance, the police told me. The car was registered in my name too. I had an overdrawn bank account. There was a bad prairie loan. A lien on a leased Ford pickup. In Alberta, his entire life had become my life. He was living under the name Gabriel English. It was as if he never expected me to live a life, so he'd better do it for me.

Lustral

I am walking through a graveyard. I am thinking of how you fall out of love and then there are, of course, elements you miss. Traces of a woman remain and you can yearn for those traces for years. Is it as banal as phrases of song stuck in your head?

I was thinking this as sharp corners of groceries dug at my legs. The path melting, leaving compressed ice from footsteps. I hope I'm describing this accurately: compressed snow in the shape of footprints. The density makes it linger when all else melts. One could get a sunburn today. Compression is this life's new religion. Pack life in. Compact.

I am looking at a handsome gravestone nestled beneath twin Carolina pine. Simple. Where Nan Brennan and her husband are buried. There is a birthdate and a dash for Nan. Snow on the stone's shoulders. The birth and dash make me realize the elemental traces of love.

Lines of ice fall from telephone wires and sizzle against the pavement. Sunlight races through streaks of cloud. I had seen Nan in a snowbank near a red mailbox. She was sitting awkwardly, her legs sticking straight out. She had a resigned hunch in her shoulders. On her lap a brown paper bag. She shouldnt be sitting in the snowbank. I was walking home from my carrel at the university.

Gabe, that you?

Nan?

I feel froze.

Her legs are thick. There is a slight burgundy colour to the flesh. I try helping her up but she feels better sitting. It's great that she said Gabe.

I stand in the road and a car swerves past. A second car.

An abstract longing is hard to describe. I have known men to take eight years to leave a woman. At least I have been decisive. But I fell into Femke as easily as I fell out of Doris. Though the two are not interchangeable.

Doris. There was not enough to love. I never loved enough. There was always an absence that stood above me with its arms crossed.

I say to Nan Brennan, I am seeing Femke now.

Who?

Femke. Her parents are Dutch, but she grew up in Ontario.

Denmark.

No, the Dutch are from Holland. You should rest.

We watch the digital meter silently rack up a red fare to Emergency.

Nan was walking home. It was nice out. Then she lost her breath and her legs grew weak. I have no Nan, so I like calling her Nan.

My lungs, she says, were filled up and I got so tired I couldnt walk any further. And I sat down on that snowbank, either that or fall down. I could feel the snow melting and it trickled down my legs. I thought it was blood.

Doris: It was congestive heart failure. Blood in her lungs. Another ten minutes and she could have frozen.

At last a taxi.

Doris, upset that no one stopped.

Me: There was a paper bag and it could have been alcohol.

Doris: It was a present.

She was sitting on her purse. People thought she was drunk.

They should have stopped.

I only stopped because I knew her. I was at my carrel all day and left at the right moment.

Carrel?

And I think of Doris, who was in chorale at high school. I thought of a pent-up place.

I have not seen Doris in six months.

Sitting in Outpatients with Doris and now her clothes look new, from hiking catalogues. She paid someone to cut her hair. I want to put my hand on her thigh. Why can't I do this.

At home Femke tries to push a hand up under my shirt.

Stop it.

Oh, come on.

We struggle in the kitchen. I drop the groceries and twist the handle of the pan so we dont knock it. We twirl, feet stomping the linoleum. Finally I freeze and Femke, from behind, has both hands pressed over my chest.

Youre late.

She directs me to the bathroom. I tell her about the grave being filled. I sit on the side of the bathtub while Femke removes a tampon. She stands, knees slightly bent, the green thread wound onto her middle finger. The pellet slips into a wad of toilet paper. She likes to squeeze the toilet paper, feel the heat of herself. She has been polite to listen of Doris and Nan.

She must have been buried the weekend. And Doris never told you.

I stroke Femke along the line of her thigh but she doesnt lean into me. Perhaps she knows that if we speak Doris's name I must picture her, and who wants a sexual touch blurred in with a memory of another. It's true that I try to compare, but I can't. I think this must be a failing of the imagination. All women have become Femke, or is it that the physical doesnt matter, or do I have a dull memory. I know I am attracted, physically, to Femke.

There is a fleeting image of Doris's collar bones, a chain gently slapping. An adjustment under my legs. The meeting, of chests parting. I can pick out detail, a particular expression, how she inhales, fragments remain thin as dreams. The softness of stomachs touching. I had grown to like Doris's body, but this is something you should never learn. A rasp of hair on legs. The first time, a giggle of disbelief that this is happening. I watched Doris, shyly, remove her bra with her shirt still on. Her arms disappearing into her shirt, the removal. A bare, close gaze without glasses. A shivered line across a thigh; the salt trace of sleep. This is all minor and caught in the corner of my eye. To be in the present is never peripheral.

It is as if I am sleeping with versions of these women. But the memories are fading the further in time they fall.

I make a short list of the women I have slept with. I squint to remember what they looked like. I can never remember more than a three-second interval. What does it matter? But I think there is something to this. The body a bookmark, the more you remember the more youve read.

After supper I fold the bedsheets and take out the winter flannel. There is a faint stain on the sheet. I realize this is left from Doris's period. From last winter. Washed out to a grey topographical line. I press the flannel to my face. I had read about Cook in my carrel: that it is easier to discover something exists than it is to discover something does not exist. That something, I am realizing, can be a continent, or love.

Almost asleep. Femke under the sheets. The sheets mould her form, toes pointing up. I am glad she is tall and strong. It is flesh but it is Femke. In her sleep she touches herself. From the side, my cock peeling her with the sound of an orange. Squeezing her nipples. She likes this. There is a dream and I am accompanying her.

Femke says there is nothing like the soft penetration of warm water. You can get the pebbles of water drumming on a precise spot. She has a vibrator. It is the size of two C-cell batteries, white plastic with a rounded tip. In bed she packs in the batteries and the buzz is like an electric shaver. She places it against her labia. I am excited by her wants, her physical secrets she expresses confidently. Femke pleasuring herself in the shower. She will take the shower nozzle off the wall and lie on the bathtub floor. Her back on an inflatable plastic pillow. Is there a greater trust than to let a man watch you?

I look up onanism. When Onan felt the pulse in the root of his cock, he withdrew and ejaculated. I will love her and have sex with her, but I will not come inside her.

I will not raise my brother's seed.

For this Onan was killed.

I went to the hospital. A nurse said it didnt look good. Nan had a tube up her nose, tied to a trolley of machines. Doris reading paperwork in the waiting area. Her father in a car accident. Her mother from a brain tumour. Doris can remember visiting her mother. Doris: Mom said take care of yourself. She never said my name.

Her aunt with four kids already, so Doris moved to a friend of the family. Doris the eldest of five. Mrs Tuttle saying, Where's the twelve-year-old.

Doris slept in the basement on a cot by the furnace. You could watch the flame flicker. She made it into a friend. You could swing this circle of metal over and watch the oil get eaten.

Then Nan and Pop Brennan took her over. Doris would walk the garden with Nan, holding a map to the flowers. The map was a coloured key that noted the shifts in bloom. The colours changing from month to month so there was always a fresh flower to spy in the morning.

Nan Brennan is saying she doesnt want to be cremated. She wants to leave her bones in the earth. She was born with a caul and she's had luck ever since. She had been working on a hooked rug and asks Doris to finish it. Flat colours of red, green and white. The cut cloth from Pop's old clothes. She asks me if I want anything.

The last visit I made with Doris. When we were going out. It was after a chimney fire. It was spring, when shells of old ice cover the gardens. Nan kept a slow burn in the woodstove. Creosote in the chimney had ignited. Instead of pouring hoses on the house the firemen had asked, politely, for styrofoam cups. They filled one with water and nimbly climbed the roof, gently dropping the cup down the chimney. Then another. A new fireman arrived and asked how many cups it took.

On the bathroom wall above her Bible a faded sepia photo of four men holding a large tuna by the tail. None looks like Pop Brennan. The faces are ecstatic, as if they had caught the fish by accident. The fins like a backbone. I had asked how old the photo was and Nan had peered at it as if for the first time.

Oh, it must be thirty years old, she said.

How long's it been on the wall?

Oh, longer than that.

The doctor: She'll be in for another week.

Doris stayed at Nan's and she invited us both over. I said to Femke, You can meet her. Femke stood tall and confident by the kitchen sink. She said, Can you understand why I'd rather not? This surprises me. I say, Should I go? She says, Go. Do you want me to encourage you to go? I'm not comfortable, she says.

Doris: I was only in town for the weekend and now it's been two weeks. The kids are vibrant and the community is strong because of oil development. She has bought a skidoo.

You're happy with Femke?

Yes.

I can't tell Doris I think of her. I left her. It would be impudent to say I think of her. So I just agree that I'm happy. The intimate things you build with someone do not translate to a new person.

Doris: I knew when I left that you would get together with Femke. I could feel it.

I had lived alone for three months. I spent six days a week in the library. I met Femke in a graduate course. She had just arrived in Newfoundland, was here by default. She had applied to universities on both coasts and only Memorial had accepted her.

Femke gave a presentation that impressed me. I could see she had passion. She accepted my invitation to the Breezeway. I wanted a roommate and Femke wasnt allowed to smoke where she was.

But it was all shyness and practical matters. Rent, for instance.

At the end of summer I invited Femke to my parents' cabin. Get out of the city, see some woods. We hitchhiked and it's easy. People assumed we were a couple, which, secretly, excited both of us. We played cribbage and read Edgar Allan Poe. The flax and monkshood. A fire on the beach for hotdogs and a tin of beans. I try swimming but the water cuts me at the hips. I towel off by the fire and Femke rubs my neck. We find faces in the coals. There are blankets for both beds, but I suggest sleeping together. Even with this there is mere friendship, practicality, intended.

I can feel the heat of her body, the vague profile of her hip against the wall. The Coleman lantern throbbing low.

Can I kiss you, she asks.

The strength of her bare arms around my back. She presses away all the space. There is a gentle noise in the rafters, as if a lynx is on the roof. I have never seen a lynx. Femke presses my hand between her legs. A wet glint of finger.

The sound is coming from inside. It could be a sparrow or a squirrel. I shine the flashlight to the noise and catch the arced wings of a small bat. It hangs directly above us. It yawns, showing a huge pink mouth. It is brilliant in its small brown perfection. I click off the light and press. The texture, the shape, completely different from Doris. Femke is shaking. The bone in her hip is excited. Her eyes are stitched, as if someone has told her to make a wish. Her skin tingling in the low light, that snowy light of darkness. It is a body completely unlike any body I have slept with.

The bat scratches above us. The tremor builds into a low short grunt, a slight drawing in of the hips. Femke's chest begins to mottle, her jaw stretched open. She says, I'm sensitive, just wait. She opens her legs a little. She is very warm.

When I lie back a pain hits my stomach. Sit up, she says. I have to stand. I have to stand and walk. I walk downstairs with the flashlight. The lake is a blue strip from the moon. The pain is fine wires probing my gut. I try juggling the pain, but it pierces each organ. I manage to open the front door and vomit on the concrete step.

The ground is cold and I have to feel over the roots of trees. My toes are like roots. A bat brushes my hair. I negotiate the path to the outhouse. I immediately shit out a spray and keep the door open to throw up again. I prop the door open with my foot for ventilation. The sky is black and the deep spruce reach over me. I take very short, quick breaths. My skin is buzzing, like a struck funny bone. My arms and legs feel numb, as if the circulation is cut off. On the rough planks of the outhouse door, a shadow of an arm, a clenched hand with one finger aimed at the ground. The shadow is sinewy as if tense with muscles. It is the hand of God saying: You are going to hell. It stretches down off the sky nailed to the spruce and falls on the door. I lean against the toilet paper and decide, I do not want to die in an outhouse in central Newfoundland.

I take quick short steps back to the cabin and fall on my parents' bed. Femke says, Do you want a blanket. I know she is calmly half hysterical. But I dont want anything. A pan is set beside the bed. She covers me in a blanket. As soon as I feel the blanket I want another. And another. Femke piles eight blankets on me and I want more. I want the pain pressed out. I wonder if Femke can drive a standard, get me to a hospital in the dark. But she has no idea where we are. We are two turnoffs from the highway. It isnt until the morning that I remember that I had thought this, never spoke aloud, and that we had hitchhiked here. I wriggle on the bed until the sky turns blue and the sun reaches out of the east like a hand.

You think it's a sign, dont you.

Me: It was food poisoning.

Nan is released after sixteen days.

Femke, when she moved in, had said: This place is a shrine. Youve got Doris everywhere.

There were photos and drawings. Letters. A cushion she'd made. Her scarf. Slowly, I packed Doris away. But she persisted into ordinary objects, items we had shared. The nightshirt. A favourite frying pan. The sheets. A jade tree.

A week before Christmas Femke takes me bowling. There is something alien in wearing rented shoes. I learn to do the scoring. Femke bowls a strike and the pins are lifted by transparent filaments. On the walls are painted pins with the looming shadow of a ball approaching.

On the way home we see an orange glow above the houses. We watch Dominion burn. We join the audience held back by yellow police tape. Femke has never seen flames as high. First, the Church Lads' Brigade, three storeys of century-old wood.

The towers orange before they cave in. Flames cross the road, licking the fish-and-chips restaurants. There are Christmas lights in the trees. Fire trucks douse the fish and chips with thick hoses. Flames reach out to touch utility poles. Wires crackle. A transformer explodes. Streetlights vanish with a sizzle. Now only light from the fire.

Dominion catches and the advertisements for tomatoes shrivel. Turkeys and ducks cook in their freezers. The restaurants across the street catch. Propane tanks in back explode, sending flame shooting up like orange fountains. There is a roar of boiling fat. Flame hits Long's Hill. The entire downtown is threatened, everything depends on the wind. People are being evacuated. I know Nan Brennan will be among them. You can see chairs, televisions, lamps, couches, halfway out front doors. Into hatchbacks and pickups. Water streams down Long's Hill, freezing in thick tongues. Cinder chunks drift over the shingles of downtown. We hear their light thud on the roof of K & K Convenience. In bed I can still feel the heat of the fire on Femke's face.

In the morning automatic hoses dump water into deep bottoms of steaming buildings. The air bright and raw. You see new architecture, what was stone and brick. Icicles hang from a network of charred pipes. Ice on everything. What was black is white. Vinyl siding on the south side of Long's Hill has buckled. The clapboard is fine. The entire block encased in a sheen of ice. Windows, mailboxes, doorsteps. Then a light snow. At night the basement of Dominion breaks into flame again. As if the earth's mantle has been ruptured.

In the new year I am on my way to the library when I meet Bob Chafe in the Belvedere cemetery. He is filling a hole beside Pop Brennan. Bob is short with a puffy face and stout fingers. He stares at his feet when he speaks, then looks you in the eye as you respond.

Just putting Mrs Brennan under.

They had a ceremony this morning. The priest came. And her granddaughter. She was funny, Bob says. Mr Brennan is under that lump of snow. And the granddaughter said, I hope they dont fight down there.

About a foot from the surface there are strips of yellowed, torn plastic. Bob Chafe says they put plastic down to keep the frost out. Under a clear tarp is a pneumatic drill and a generator.

The backhoe can't get in. Needs to have its wheels on grass.

The hole cuts through three feet of dense shale, through several ages of accumulation. It is as if they are putting Nan back into her own time.

Wormholes

We were asked, How many people have you slept with. I said three. A friend at the party told this to Doris. I had only mentioned Laurie to Doris. So who else, she asked. I am one and Laurie is two. Who. And I said Beth Willis. Yes, Beth. I tell Doris that I remember nothing of my night with Beth. Hardly anything. It was before I moved to Toronto. A month before.

She says, But you were with me then.

I ask, Do you really want to hear this?

No, Gabe, I dont. But I have to hear it.

So be it. You had gone to your parents' for a visit. I met up with Beth at the university library. We were taking a night course in sociology. We went to the Breezeway and started drinking. We were splitting beers. As if that would make us less drunk. We talked about relationships. The natural state of affairs. Monogamy or polygamy. She tucked her heels up on her seat, as she did in class. Wrapped her knees with her smoking arm. Then we kissed. Beth had her mother's car. We walked across the parking lot with our eyes closed, hands held. She was parked by the duck house. Her knuckles shifting gears into downtown. At my door she asked. We had been drinking, Doris.

How did she ask? Did she say, Would you like to sleep with me? or, I want to sleep with you. I want to hear all of it, Gabe. Leave nothing out.

She said, I want to sleep with you. She took off her glasses. Held my elbows. We knelt on the bed and kissed. Beth over me, her knees flexing, her white knees and the round of her stomach and her small breasts. I held her hips. But it's faint now.

Remember everything.

The beer kept me from coming. You know how I come quickly. And she was pleased when she saw how hard an orgasm I had with her. She went to the toilet, which you can see from the bed. She came back to bed and we lay there for a few minutes. We listened to the people upstairs argue. She smoked. She said she had to go. I said you can stay. I can make you an egg. But she got up and all that nakedness.

And you mean to say, Gabe, that this affair doesnt affect you? I hardly think about it.

And yet you remember such detail.

Love and hate are neighbours. They are rooms with a thick retaining wall between them. The wall is a tough barrier to penetrate. As time curves on its belly and touches back on itself. There are wormholes in space that connect, but one must be searching for these holes. These corridors through which one can transport. For love to turn into hate, one must be looking for that very possibility. One must be amenable to the occurrence.

If we held marks on our body from the things we leave behind, perhaps our memory would not be so peaceful. We would be mottled by our own misdeeds. The danger is that evanescent marks, marks that evaporate like rain on pavement, may be noticed and fixed in another's memory, as if that state is eternal. It would be as if everyone could read minds. Remember and freeze images that, for the one who originally experienced them, have changed, or evaporated.

In Turkey they spread buckets of water over the sidewalks to keep the dust down. Do you remember this, Doris?

She says, I remember kissing Ayhan. I remember you playing chess with Bayram, and Ayhan took me to buy tomatoes. We held hands. I reached up and kissed his mouth.

History cannot be written. An experience is not limited to the one experiencing it.

A woman says to a man, Do you know what I want to do now? I want to go home and make love to my husband.

That is what Doris told Ayhan.

What goes on in the brain should be concealed.

Aristotle describes two forms of memory. There are the internal markings, the things which affect our soul, change our character. And then there are the marks on the body: scars, moles, external tokens. Odysseus, disguised as a beggarman, returns to his house. His dog, Argus, recognizes him immediately. His old nurse Eurycleia recognizes a scar on his thigh while bathing him.

Doris shapes her environment. The containers that hold her are never just right. She turns two rooms into one. She builds bookcases. She shifts the location of the basement stairs. The living room entrance is not to her liking, so she moves that. She cuts a hole through to the hallway. As she boards up the old doorway she says, We should leave messages in the wall. We draw along the beams, the gyproc. Doris writes Gabriel hates Doris and signs it Gabriel. I write Doris hates Doris and sign it Doris. I draw a portrait of us and Doris says there should be a beam between us. Then we seal the information. It is still there, locked into the wall of our house. Secret documents sewn into a jacket's lining.

Accidental marks are visible. Chosen marks we can hide, like tattoos on the shoulder. We decide when to reveal them. But accidental marks are harder to conceal. Some people can pick them up, notice them even when we think the marks have vanished or are concealed. As black holes are spotted not by their presence, but by the absence of matter.

I turn on the lights. The smell of dust burning off lit bulbs. The light over the wall with our false signatures inside. The surgeon's sutures dissolving in the bloodstream.

Doris and I were discussing how, when I write and edit, there are versions of things I omit. But these versions —

description and dialogue — which I find unnecessary, still linger in my head. I think, this passage is redundant, I will delete this. And yet the passage contains a crucial piece of information. My head thinks the information is elsewhere, but it is this passage that holds it. The rest of the text carries a memory of the information, a gap pointing to its absence.

It had been raining all week. Then one day the sun shone through the patio windows. I took the drafts of this story and placed them neatly on the gleaming white patio table and sat in the plastic chair. As I worked on revising the paragraph preceding this one I noticed the papers on the table were turning from brilliant white to dark grey. Like litmus paper. Starting from the corners working to the centre. In the bright sun. Then my brain shifts from one possibility to the other. I realize that the table top is a sheet of rainwater. The paper is soaked. And I am left with that moment of not understanding what I am experiencing.

Last winter Doris took me ice fishing. She has an ice pick her father forged. The shaft is dented with tiny hammer blows, the strength of his arms frozen into the steel. I cut a small tree from the periphery of the pond, limb it and shave the end to fit the pick. Doris uses her boot to sweep away snow. Then chop. The ice is bright on the surface. Then it turns grey. A deep granite. Finally blue. The ice is eighteen inches thick. We take turns chopping. I scoop out the ice with my leather shucks. The hole swallows my arm to the elbow. Then the ice pick pierces the water. The sound changes to a dull thunk. Water gurgles through as Doris quickly chips at the hole to make it larger. The water rising to the ice surface. There is ice residue left in the water. I take off my shuck and scoop out the ice. I pretend the water is boiling hot. That my hand is being burnt, not frozen. From the corner of my eye I can see Doris with the pick raised, as if she has forgotten that we have hit water.

On the same pond in summer we skinny dip after midnight. The wharf is wet from rain. We throw ourselves in and warm up. Doris can tread water for hours. Then she holds me, places her weight on me so that we sink. I can feel the shape of the air in her lungs as she pushes us down. Her skin is like rubber. She lets go and we rise to the surface. As we dry ourselves on the wharf, the cold of the wood sinks into the soles of our feet. I watch her glow in the light of the stars. As we walk back along the trail to the car she says the wind is like a jet of cold water through her back and the water is coursing through her, coming out of her breasts.

Femke, and His
Then Girlfriend

In bed that night he wondered. Layers of wonder. He imagined
marrying Femke. This was something he imagined with lots of
women. He knew he wouldnt marry Doris. He knew and yet
he had stayed with her. If he had said that vague thing about
being true, Doris would perhaps have nodded. He needed
rebuking. He had enjoyed stretches with Doris so much that
they turned into years, and yet every time he sat down with his
thoughts he grew tight with anxiety about Doris.

His then girlfriend still called. There are some trees, Doris
said. Skidoos stuck in the mud. In the store one banana just
like any banana and right now she has a cauliflower in the
fridge. Doris bought nine pears for eight dollars.

When he'd seen her off at the airport. Tears near the metal
detector. Then Doris stiffened and said, Oh, you know what I

forgot — my contraceptive foam.

It was over between them. A shift in geography had ended it. He didnt have the guts to leave her.

Doris had asked him to come with her. He could write in the house heated with imported oil. It was the first time geography had insisted on a decision, and it helped. He was so indecisive. This was the first thing to change, to become more decisive.

Femke had said, It's not that simple. I put up a front when I talk to my adviser. My best friend in high school used to throw her body away. You just can't say, blithely, be true to yourself.

They were drinking a box of beer on a pitched roof overlooking Water Street and Gabriel had begun with a vague philosophy. Their reflection in the big bank mirrors and grey strips of morning in the narrows.

You caught that fish in a ditch, she says.

It was a river.

You could jump across it.

It's called Virginia River.

Femke had seen him down by the lake. She'd slowed her motorbike — a bike he never got to ride, not even as a passenger — beeped. And Gabriel produced this fat trout from his coat pocket, a German brown that covered all his fingers. In some way Femke was this German brown.

They finished the beer and had black coffee at Classic Café. They decided to split a bacon lettuce and tomato. He liked that she had these tastes. Then they walked up the hills to home. She in no way approached him physically and he knew, in subtle ways, that he had.

Tearing back the tinfoil, pockets of steam. Rosemary and lemon across a speckled back.

A bee is boiling on a rose.

Gabriel is reading a letter from Doris. She describes a court case: the dance hall is temporarily the courtroom. The defence lawyer sitting under a disco light. The alleged infractions took place at the dance. In this very room. The prosecution says, And you, sir, were standing by the bar. And the attorney can't help but gesture towards the bench.

They play pool at the Cottage Inn. One lamp striking a soft cone over the blue cloth. A man with his jeans tucked into his white socks, as if he rode a bike.

I'm George, he says. We got the table first.

Femke slaps seventy-five cents on the table. Two women are playing two men. Pairs.

Femke says, Youre my husband, okay?

And Gabriel likes that.

She has long brown hair crinkled like bent wire. When she was young she'd wear the head of an old mop in bed. She'd always wanted long hair. Her parents were building a house to sell but something happened and they had to move in. It wasnt finished and they never got around to it. Always that house half built. Naked gyproc. The yellow studs around the porch windows.

She remembers undressing and someone at her window. But they must have been on a ladder. And there was no ladder.

Her brother would make monkeys out of his knees, she remembers that.

While drinking beers and waiting for the table, the ease of her, the understanding. Gabriel touched her arm several times and, when they left, he opened the door for her. I put my hand between her shoulder blades to guide us up the road, he remembers thinking that. The maple leaves were big and just about to be eaten.

Femke was with her friends Brenda Hogan and Carol Delaney. Gabriel had met up with them at the Ship where Femke was drinking a Corona with a slice of lime. Brenda and Carol were touching empty gin glasses. They were all smoking and Gabriel knew that Brenda and Carol were thinking about him and Femke. Both Brenda and Carol knew him when he was with Doris, but they held no allegiance to Doris. They were now Femke's friends. This was no slight towards Doris — they would still love Doris if she were in town. It was, in fact, a comfort that Doris's friends could like Femke as well.

They were smoking and he realized he had never gone out with a smoker.

The four of them went for burgers, garlic bread and two plates of mussels.

They take a skinny dip in Three Pond Barren after midnight. Hauling off his socks, he watches her prepare to dive, her glowing back against the dark trees. Standing on the cold wharf, arms out. Her hair falling to the fifth vertebra. But she has thick ankles. Remember she has those ankles.

What defined ankles Doris had!

The night did not offer definition. Gabriel could only see Femke's outline, as if his eyesight was bad. The water numbing the backs of his arms. Femke floats to the other side, only her voice left to him. Her voice is strong and she's a good swimmer.

Femke hands him a ticket to a bowling fundraiser and he watches her engage the aisle, hold the ball to her chin with her wrists touching.

But she lets out a high childish giggle and flickers one eyelid. Proverb: Mannerisms that annoy, mean something is awry.

The sleeping together. They rumble towards it and only after the act does it seem inevitable. Life's actions culminate in retrospect. They announce the fact to Brenda and Carol. But no one is surprised. This too deflates him.

Gabriel is in bed reading *From a Seaside Town*. He is surprised when Norman Levine uses the phrase 'She wouldnt fuck'. And then later the word 'cunt'. He tells this to Femke. She likes the word cunt. She thinks Gabriel is shocked because he expects Levine to be innocent of this badness. She'd been to supper at Carol's and Carol had repeated what Gabriel had said about Dr Ayres — he drives me up the effing wall. Femke: That you said ef and not fuck and they all thought that was wonderful.

She says, derisively, Carol thinks youre an angel.

Gabriel understands that this aggravates her.

Haydn and the rain on the dogberries.

He says, I'm really glad I'm with you.

It's very hard not to sound corny as you say these things and he can tell it annoys Femke because her shoulders are stiff. In the shower she spreads a gel over his chest and they rub softly together.

But tonight she decides to sleep downstairs.

They stay together throughout the fall and Christmas. And in January Gabriel accumulates some notes. He has come to some conclusions. That Femke takes things to have bad intentions. He acts up as a cry for approval, when all he's doing is trying to be funny. There's no ulterior motive, or, if there is, it is negated by the fact that he wants people to be happy. He thinks she wants him to be more serious, but if he was, she'd quickly call him dour and lose interest. She has a wacko perception of events. He used a dogberry bush for a Christmas tree. And he turned a red oven mitt into a decoration. She thinks he's not sensitive to her Christmas away from home. Gabe's feeling? That she doesnt like him receiving attention when acting silly. That he has some need for an audience, he seeks it — and approval — through it. As if he spends his waking hours concocting this image to be liked. He writes. Then it's his relationships. It irks him that Femke has a false notion of his intentions. He can imagine her talking about all this to

Brenda or anyone — laying on this fantasy — but he shouldnt be concerned about this. That is vain. He suspects his hand gestures annoy her.

He realizes that she has a thick mainland accent, and the way she says words bugs him. It doesnt even matter what she says. He is shocked by his own intolerance.

Carol and Brenda are over for lunch. To see them in the kitchen with pita bread and tofu leftovers. He sits in the living room to read, but can't help overhearing.

I called up my father, Brenda says, to ask for one good reason not to kill Mike. And he couldnt think of one. He said, Use a shotgun rather than a knife. Mom couldnt listen.

Carol: I went out with a guy once, I travelled five hundred miles every weekend to see. He would put on supper and in ten minutes it would be cooked. He loved vegetables. Was a vegetarian. He'd take a toke and that would knock him out until noon next day. He had a son who was thirty, who was getting married for the third time. Karl had never been married.

Femke mentions a platonic affair with a man in Kingston named Derek Cushion. She thinks it rose above a sexual relationship. That sex would have caused tensions and inevitably destroyed the relationship.

Gabriel: I think youre less tense with someone youre attracted to after youve slept together.

They are sitting at the moorings to the harbour. It's that darkness where the principals switch shades. Sky dark and land light. Femke says, I have a strange notion of relationships. I had a pregnancy scare at fourteen.

A man on the wharf drops his shorts and stands naked in front of them. Then the harbour patrol arcs its high beam upon them, the naked man eclipsed.

Femke asks Gabe if he ever did the bars.

No.

She used to pick up guys.

Do you remember the sex? Each partner?

Pretty much. I've always looked for self-confidence. Men all begin that way. But as soon as I'm with them they crumble, they want to put their head on my shoulder and be coddled.

You can smell the creosote off the pilings. Gabriel can tell by her alert back that she doesnt want to be touched. He wouldnt mind touching her now.

I remember Brenda asking me when my last boyfriend was, and I said three years ago. I forgot completely that I was living with a guy before I came here. I couldnt remember his name. I was sleeping with him a week before I met you.

She was with a gang when she was seventeen.

My first boyfriend, Chico, tried to keep me out. He was eventually charged with stabbing a man twenty-seven times, castrating him. The man's wife had a contract out on him. I was depressed over that, and I thought about it, using drugs, just to make people see. But atheism means you wouldnt be aware of remorse.

She went to Denmark and stayed with her grandparents for

a year. Her grandfather let two budgies out of their cage in the morning. They would perch on the arms of his glasses while he ate breakfast. Femke was crushed when he said, during a dispute, Youre just a woman.

Stories like this make Gabriel warm up and love.

Doris is in town. She is escorting a fifteen-year-old girl back to Davis Inlet. She asks to stay at the house. So Gabriel tells her about Femke.

I dont care, she says. Just dont be kissy kissy in front of me.

They have lunch at the Oasis and Carol is there with Tim Lush. Gabriel decides Tim is stocky, artificial, with a despicable Ontario accent. He realizes a lot of Femke's friends are mainlanders. He doesnt give a shit what Carol will say to Femke.

They find a yard sale at the back of Bar None. The zealot is there with his German shepherd at the top of the stair. He is drinking tea and his cuffs are unbuttoned. Gabriel remembers that the man had cautioned him on *Franny and Zooey*. He is selling shirts, glasses, pots and broken chairs. Gabriel buys a record cleaner, which the zealot used to sweep pool tables. Doris notices a tombstone up on the steep bank.

The zealot says, It's in honour of the men they hanged at Gibbets Hill. They threw their bodies in Deadman's Pond. I used an ironing board to symbolize their poverty, wrote it incorrectly for illiteracy, and painted a red rose to connote the cruelty of their fate.

It's a good idea, an ironing board.

Artificial flowers planted at the base.

When we get home Femke is in the kitchen. She doesnt flinch.

Femke, last night: I want you alert in the mornings if you want a coffee. I want to talk cogently for ten to fifteen minutes in the dawn. Gabriel: I can't guarantee that.

In short, she is saying she'd prefer to read in the kitchen with the sun during that time. That Gabriel offers no reason to have her come back to bed. Gabriel: I like the coffee, but sometimes I'm very tired. But I dont mind if youre in the kitchen.

There's sun in my room too. It banks off the bookcase and all the spines look promising.

Femke makes a face at this. She would like Gabriel to go to sleep when she does and wake up at a decent hour. But he has no outside reason to get up in the morning. He often used to work until three in the morning. Into the solid core of the world's sleep. But he lies beside Femke as she dreams, with just the forty-watt lamp on. He didnt mention the bed . . . that they have to sleep in his (hers is too narrow). It would be so much simpler, she said, if we lived apart. We could screw and then go our separate ways. He is surprised at how carnally she is taking this relationship. As if time apart would solve things.

While this was meant as a light thing to say, he feels Femke does mean it. His feeling is, anything Femke does for Gabriel, she resents it if he doesnt:

(a) immediately repay her in some way

(b) there is no b.

She ignores or forgets or is oblivious to any compromises

he makes (i.e., sleeping in his bed, not working until four a.m., reading in low wattage, etc.). She sees any demand as a real drag, why the fuck should I do it. As if they werent in love and shouldnt do things for each other.

Gabriel spends all Saturday with Doris. They drive out to see icebergs. She speaks of writing with the left hand. Having people spend a few minutes with one person and then introducing that person to the group. She describes a desire for Mr Kirk Peach. A wily, married man in his forties. At the same time another social worker is seeing Mr Peach's twenty-two-year-old son. She says Carol and Mike are getting a divorce, and Carol's interested in Tim Lush. And Brenda wants a Yeats man instead of a man who reads Yeats.

Gabriel says he watched television with Femke and Carol and Mike and Brenda and was amazed at how into the TV culture they all were. Dismayed, perhaps. For over three hours they maintained a banter over commercials, serials. They were experts. Remembering seventies culture, jingles. Mike noticing any conversation that could be turned sexual. It bored me, Gabe says, how they seemed to be at home with it.

Doris: You have to listen to what's in your heart of hearts.

In bed. Femke: I used to share bunks with my brother. We would speak through a flexible pipe. Thomas had a flashlight and he'd shine it down the pipe, but I could never see the light. I anticipated the light, but it never came. Just the glow of Tom's palm over the mouth of the pipe.

Gabriel: My brother and I called each other Joe. We still do. And it's because of the G.I. Joe dolls we played with. It was the dolls calling out to each other and somewhere along the way it transferred over to us.

They wake when a man next door slams the wall hard, making a woman cry. Three frames fall off the wall. Gabriel is tight for half an hour, but Femke falls asleep easily. And to the bathroom creeps Doris. Her soft blue shoulder growing dark against the window.

Femke has no interest in seeing Doris off at the airport.

The last night they are together they play pool with Dana. Dana is from Kingston, has a master's in early childhood development. She grew up with Femke. Dana talks and refers to her own talking, which annoys Gabriel. One should talk and not make others feel like they arent talking enough.

She asks: Are you offended when we say Newf?

She uses we.

Gabriel, politely: Not the way you say it. But I prefer Newfoundlander.

Femke: But that's hard to say, you'll admit.

And he realizes he is very far away from these women. He says, I find it easy to say. A beautiful rolling word. It's when people say it with malice.

Harold commanding the pool table. He's spent thirteen years in jail for stealing. Sold fifty pounds of meat at the bar tonight.

Stole it from Sobey's. You can get me put right back in

the pen if you call the cops now — I'm not supposed to be drinking.

He wants their support.

I'm going, Harold says, on a hunger strike. To protest how the public views welfare. That people have to feel humiliated. To be on it.

Dana: Harold, it's your responsibility to take care of yourself, no one else's. I'll support you if you help yourself.

Harold turns to Femke and asks for her shirt.

I won't give you my shirt unless youre going to put it to good use.

So Harold ignores her.

Femke: He wants to drag us to where he's at.

Earlier, Gabriel had walked to Churchill Square for garlic. He had heard the rain in the grass but could not feel it. He bought everything but the garlic. He'd seen Femke in the Dominion but did not approach her. He'd wanted to see her perform in the world without him. He watched her head for the vegetables. She picked up garlic. She knew they needed garlic.

In bed Femke says her brother had a gargoyle in his neck. He would hold his breath and bulge his neck. She said she might have a genital wart so Gabriel shouldnt go down on her. He doesnt say anything and he's convinced his pause is the same as shouting youve got a what. She had them years ago and it feels like one has returned. It was with a man who was a friend of her father's. He was an actor and he had to masturbate before he had sex with her, otherwise he'd come too early. As she tells him this he strokes her to climax, twice.

She says she's never had that done to her before. Only self-stimulation. She's never managed to orgasm to penetration solely.

In the morning they build a slow argument over an article in a magazine. Femke: You put down everything I have to say. Gabriel disputes this: I merely offer a counter to things you declare as truth. Femke adds, Right? to the end of all her statements. Gabriel: No, that's not right. I dont agree.

He leaves when she says I know what youre going to say. He says, You always cut me off.

But she won't resolve the issue. Is sleeping in her room. For her, it's a matter of him saying No, youre wrong. He thinks, or at least his intention is, to say, Well, couldnt it be otherwise? here's a possibility. She doesnt like hearing him come up with refutations. And fine if it spoils her attempt to arrive at a theory.

She plays her music loud, and he knows she's in bed reading comics. How can I be with a woman who reads comics? She bangs her desk, and yells, after a fight.

Gabriel returns Levine to the library. He eats cheese on toast with sliced tomato and rosemary. Femke is in the shower. She says, I didnt get much sleep, I was worried. His footsteps were at three in the morning. He says, I smelled the exhaust from your motorbike this morning. Through my window. She says, I've decided to sleep Monday nights separate. He says, I saw a man at the library counting squares of orange carpet. She says, Did you hear?

He says, I heard. He says, It seems a strange thing to think of sleeping with you. Right now it seems the strangest thing to imagine.

Gabriel's brother Junior phones from Daytona. He wants to get backing for a Daytona car. Gabriel compares his brother's dreams to Lindbergh's. Junior says there's a huge teak sailing boat that got wrecked in the Bahamas over the weekend and they should go down and salvage it and sail it to St John's and sell it for a lot of songs.

He says, Also, Gabe, I want information from Doris about the cost of land in Labrador.

Gabriel tells him Doris is catching char in the harbour with the natives. She attended a wedding and someone honked the only truck horn in Davis Inlet to make the groom feel at home. The groom from Gander.

Junior says, Gander Gander where can I land her.

Gabriel tells his brother nothing about Femke.

Second Heart

They go in Lady Slipper Road and hunt with the truck, cab
lifting over potholes. Because the father's feet are bad. Splash in
wheel wells and tilt and lean into each other. It's an intimate,
unintentional touch of shoulders and knees. They haul off by a
small pond the shape of a knife and pull back the red vinyl seat
and dislodge two twelve gauges and a Winchester pump and
load up. The father instructs.

Only a bull, Gabe. If there's no antlers you leave it. If
Junior's with you, let him shoot. I want this to be legal. You've
got to be close to use a slug. Remember how far from the road
you are. Dont go in miles. Keep the slugs separate. If you have
a shell in the chamber, keep it breached. Your barrel needs
bluing, Gabe.

A box of food from Mom all stacked to get the most out of
a cardboard box, enough food really for three days but then

Junior is with them.

Junior: Meat pie looks like it's going off.

Dad: Yeah, better eat it now. Sausage rolls, too.

Youre right. That roast chicken, dont forget that.

It's Junior first as he has eyes that see into the periphery always, he sees black lifting wings near the pond. They eat the pie and walk to it, Junior with the rifle and the crows hop and lift and are annoyed. They haul away heavy from the bloated guts and front half of a moose. The carved white hind quarters, flayed.

Someone in a hurry.

The poachers had taken steaks, roasts. Carved them quick off the bone.

The father tries to turn the carcass with his boot but it rocks back into its own hollow. What a waste.

About a hundred pounds of meat.

There's disdain in his tight mouth.

Junior's eye now, roving, frozen on a cutover. Gabriel follows the eye to a mound of dead alders. But the branches are moving and as he concentrates the branches slowly separate into finer branches and antlers and the heads of three moose. There is only one with antlers. Junior already with the sights on him. The white bone of his cheek pressed to the stock. A shot hard on the air and the bull reels, his neck lowers and swings.

The cows.

Leave them, June.

Junior hesitates on the two cows. He sights, says quietly, Bang. He pivots the rifle three degrees, again says, Bang. But his trigger finger doesnt squeeze. He looks for the bull, but can't find it through the scope.

Is it down?

Dad: It went behind the rise. You got him, now just leave him be.

The two cows stare straight at them, downwind, calm, lifting their noses. Now turn and trot quickly, shoulders full of alarm but almost haughty.

Junior is running through high brush, rifle at the top of his arm, he sinks out of sight. There are three more shots. Gabe and his father make the rise and see Junior sizing up the strain and falter.

Dad: Dont go hitting the meat, June.

One cow on the knoll looking back. Hesitates.

Could get her, Dad.

You leave it.

The bull in deadfall.

Junior: They love to get into that. You shoot one in the open and he runs for the alders.

If you'd let him be.

Junior paces around the shoulders of the animal. He takes his time looking for a spot. Well, that was quick, hey? He positions the muzzle of the rifle to the ear and fires and all four legs lift a little then strike the ground and relax. Junior pulls a knife from the back of his belt and tucks it under the throat. He rummages until a red gush pours over his hand.

The cow still lingers, nostrils flared, understanding all through her nostrils.

Remember the time when the eyes popped out, Dad? I was putting one through the ear, Gabe, and the force. Junior laughs. Held on by stringy things to the sockets.

Dad: That was ugly.

The cow turns and leaves.

They wait over the throat of the animal. They pass time by looking at the truck with its high cap on the woods road and the gap on the hill where the cow was last and understanding the lay of the woods road, which weaves through pulp mill cutover and heads to the highway. Then they begin the paunch. The father says I wonder where that second cow got to. He knots a length of seat belt strap around one hoof and pulls it wide so the moose is splayed. He ties this to a stump left by the Company. Junior punctures the belly and works the blade along, piercing a white membrane but not the stomach. A steam rises. His blade runs smoothly through the hide like a zipper. Blood sloshes into the cavity. Junior counts the ribs, Here, Dad.

They carve sideways between the third and fourth ribs. Hot blood leaks out the sides. They rock the moose to empty it of blood. The stomach like an island in the blood, the yellow of chanterelles.

Junior approaches the head again. He cuts through backbone and slices the gullet. He works off the head and tosses it on some low bushes. One brown eye staring back at the body. If the eyes are closed it's still alive.

They return to the cavity, chopping through the boiled egg

of sternum to pry open ribs. They coax the vast stomach down, slicing hitches that anchor it to bone.

Let's get him on his side more.

They roll out the guts. The father ties off the dark intestine with a rope and then separates the anus.

Where's the scrotum.

It's out already.

You should have left it on.

You dont want that, Dad.

You do want it, June.

I tossed it off in some bushes.

He wheels around, points with the knife.

Over there somewheres.

Gabriel checks the bushes and finds a strip of hide and the loose orange balls. He holds it up.

That's it.

He puts it up by the head.

Junior reaches into the chest, his shirt sleeves pushed up. The motion indicates he is cutting something, hoses. His hands appear with the heart. It is bigger than the platter of his hands. His silver watch smeared in blood.

In my bag, he says.

Gabriel finds the newsprint and Junior lays the heart on it beside the scrotum. He is careful with the heart. He wipes his hands front and back in the gorse and then up and down the thighs of his jeans.

I'm just going to see what's down there, Junior says.

Dad: Youre not taking the rifle.

Junior: I emptied it. I just want to use the scope.

The father wipes out the ribcage with grass. Take a shotgun.

I'll take a shotgun too.

Well, make sure the action's empty.

It's empty. I'm waiting for some shotgun ammo, man.

The father hands him shells, for birds.

They rest while Junior investigates the knoll. He is holding the rifle to look through the scope. Gabe and his father fall back onto the spring of alders. Look around. The father takes out a flask. He says, He's not supposed to do that.

It's dangerous.

There could be a cartridge. Dont do that, will you. Want some?

Gabriel takes the flask, but it's iced tea.

Good isnt it. I can't abide pop.

They have the pond to get round and then a bog to the road. From this angle the bog and pond are only long slivers of what they are. The wheelbarrow is in the truck. And Junior returns.

You see anything?

The mill got it all logged. Not a feather anywhere. You'll have to figure out a good route for us, Gabe.

Junior notices the head and picks up his axe. He puts his foot on the nose to steady it. Then he hacks into the skull. When he swings, the butt of the axe nearly touches Gabriel's ear. The axe leaves blunt wedges in the skull, white showing through like coconut. They are sprayed with skull and brain.

Sorry about that. I should be doing this over here.

Junior drags the head by one antler to the side.

Gary wants the rack, he says.

The father waves Gabe back and they wait until the antlers are free. It's a small set of antlers, about eight points.

The bull last year was huge, hey Dad. Had four sprigs coming down over his eyes before the plate even started.

Junior puts his thumb to his cheek, fingers stretched out, to indicate the plate.

Gabriel finds a grown-over trail from a tree harvester, right to the road. He brings up the wheelbarrow. And watches his father carve out the lower jawbone. He has trouble getting through the hinge.

Let me at that, Dad.

Junior aims the axe at the hinge.

Watch the back teeth, June.

You want it here?

Just back.

When the jawbone is off Junior wraps the scrotum around it and reserves it by the heart. So they won't lose any of it.

The scrotum to identify the sex. You keep that in the freezer for if the police come. The jawbone for Wildlife.

There is a blue dumpster outside the Irving gas station, a heap of skinned lower jawbones.

They saw off the legs above the talus and place them in a row. The father scalps a strip of hide off the spine. Gabe picks up the saw.

Junior: An axe is faster, Gabe.

Dad: Sawing is preferable.

Junior: You can tap an axe through and not splinter.

I like a clean cut, June.

They hold the front half while Gabriel saws. They pry open the quarters as the teeth descend, so the brace of the saw doesnt catch. Gabriel wipes the backbone clean to make sure he's straight. The bone is warm. He wouldnt have thought bone had heat.

Dad: That's a fine animal, June.

Yes, fine animal. Those cows were fine too.

Each quarter a hundred pounds easy. The father takes out the silver tags.

Now Dad not yet.

It was supposed to be first thing.

Sure Dad we almost got this animal out.

June. We're tagging it.

He punctures a leg between tendon and bone.

Okay Dad. Thread em through but dont click em.

We've been through this, June.

Dad, it's only ten minutes to the truck.

And twenty to the highway and an hour to home. In my truck. On my licence.

The father stands. Looks Junior in the eye. With your mother. That licence is between you and your mother, and your mother won't have it.

Sure, Mom dont need to know.

First thing she'll look for when it's hanging in the building. How come there's no tags.

We'll hang it over at Gary's.

June, I'm not having anything to do with Gary. If there's no tags involved, youre alone.

As Gabe and Junior carry out a quarter in the wheelbarrow, Junior: Dad, boy. A man of details.

In the dark of the truck, a beer each, sitting on the wheel wells. The moose quarters jiggling, the meat warm. They hold on for potholes. Junior says, If I come home I can work with Dad. I can make daybeds and baby cradles. I'll get Dad to show me. Because he needs a hand, Gabe. Like this truck. He didnt understand the gas consumption. It was eating gas. And I showed him the pollution gear. Marked all the hoses and gauges with chalk and we hauled out the works.

They are sitting in the back of the truck, the father driving. The night highway moving backwards, framed by the truck cap. A car passes and the tags glint on stiff legs above the tailgate.

Dad: We'll let that hang a week.

Mom: It wasnt lying in its own blood again, was it?

Junior: It was lying in someone else's blood.

Junior slit its throat first thing.

Because if it's like that, Al, I'm not having it.

The meat's well cased.

The brothers share the bunkbeds. Junior stretches his legs and makes the frame crack and fifteen years vanish. Teenage years of Junior home late, drunk, opening the window to pee and it splashes over the desk. Urine on the blankets.

They watch headlights of cars arc over the bedroom wall.

Christmas, Junior says. If I come home I'm coming home then. I'm getting a tree and really celebrating.

What about Mom.

Gabe, I'm having a tree. I know she calls that pagan. Well, to say that is like me telling her to fuck off. It's Christ's birthday and I feel like enjoying it. And if she dont, then I'll live in Dad's building.

A little later: Gabe, eventually I want to build a little cabin with twelve-volt lighting in Mount Moriah. I want to occupy the land and I dont care what happens. I'm gonna keep the land the way I like it and have a son who can take it over. I want you to do me a favour.

Pause.

Can you do me a favour?

What.

A favour, boy.

Yes, what the fuck is it.

Look up the rules on building codes and old Newfoundland laws on occupying land. If you could get some books on it or show me where it's to.

Junior would get out of bed, leap down, and drive Gabriel with his leg. In the thighs and ribs. Gabriel vowed to hate him.

I hate you. No, you dont, he'd say. I'm your brother, you got to love me. You can't help it.

And he realizes this is true.

In the morning, Junior:

Gabe. Come on.

What's up.

We're getting Dad a load of wood.

He's got lots of wood.

Come on, Gabe. He's got bad feet. I got the saw in the truck. I got gas and oil. I even made you a little sandwich. Just half a load. We'll be done by one.

Is Dad going?

Dad can't be at that any more.

I'm too stiff.

Just you and me against some trees.

They take the truck and go in Lady Slipper Road again.

That deadfall stuff is rotten, June.

Are you catching on?

Junior parks where they were parked before. And get out. It's cold and low light. Grey rolling nimbus. Junior takes an axe from behind the seat.

Okay.

Junior: You can't guess?

A sweat creeps into Gabe's armpits.

There's a moose in there.

Junior points the axehead to the knoll.

Man oh man theyre long gone, June.

I'm not talking about the one that got away.

They walk past the bog and around the pond and the crows now at yesterday's remains. Dew wetting their jeans. The butchered head and swollen stomach. Four cut-off legs in a row. Four legs with no space between them. The respectful thing would be to give them space.

Gabriel follows Junior to the knoll. Where Junior had looked for birds. Gabe pans the clearcut. Then he sees the cow moose lying in full run in the clearing. Its throat cut.

Fuck, June.

Got her when I shot the bull. I was too quick for Dad. Aint it beautiful? Had to find it yesterday, cut its throat.

Jays are perched at the eyes.

You know what Dad does when he hits a moose, Gabe? He boils the kettle. That's what he wanted to do, boil a fucking kettle while that bull died. Moose sees you after him, he runs. If you hang back he'll lie down. He's hurt, see? Wouldnt have got this cow if we'd boiled a kettle now would we. Got to watch out for wardens, okay?

A quarter rolls off his back.

Junior: The meat is some alive, hey?

We shouldve taken the barrow.

Dad would miss it. He'd say, you took the barrow for wood?

They take a quarter each, Gabriel carrying the lighter, front quarters. Resting at the remains of yesterday's bull. Then all the way to the truck. At least there's the path the wheel barrow made. But Gabriel stops with his second quarter.

Gabriel: I say we leave it.

Okay, we leave it. But I'm getting the heart.

Junior jogs through the cutover, to the knoll, and down to cut the hoses that hold the heart to the lungs. He shuffles the heart under his arm and jogs back to Gabe.

Take the heart.

Junior hoists the last quarter over his shoulder. He strides hard for the truck.

Gabriel wraps the heart in newsprint and tucks it safe on a shelf in the cab. Junior rolls the quarter into the truck bed.

That's seventy-five dollars' worth of meat, Gabe. Couldnt let that go to waste.

Okay, the deal is you drive and I sit in back with the moose. Youre to rap on the rear window. If you see anything at all.

Gabe can spot Junior through the rear view mirror. Junior with his hands ready under a quarter. And up on the hill where the road winds down is a white jeep. Gabriel slows. The jeep disappears into the green. Junior lifts the meat over the tailgate. He has to lift and throw the meat to the side so it makes the ditch. He lifts a second quarter and hurls this too. Gabriel keeps it moving. Junior pushes down the legs on the other two quarters and drapes himself over the moose.

The warden passes. Gabriel nods to him but the warden's eye is on the back of the truck. The jeep halts in the side mirror. The warden is studying the truck. Gabriel tilts carefully through potholes. He wants the warden's brake light to wink out. He wills the red light to dampen and it does. The warden drives on. And Junior bangs on the window.

They back up and bring up the meat. The fresh bone and cut muscle stained in dirt. When they get to the highway Gabe pulls over. They cover the meat in a blue tarp and Junior gets in the passenger side. I'm beat.

There is a nasty cut across his wrist from a bone.

Couldnt get it all out in time. Dad got the fucking tailgate on. Tailgates are fucking useless.

Gabriel drives into town, up past the house and down into Curling. Junior asleep against the door post.

Junior reaches over to press the horn. Stop here, Gabe.

He jumps out and opens a screen door and disappears. He comes out with Gary. Gary is wearing a shirt that goes with a tuxedo.

Best to back her in, Gary says. Hi Gabe.

Gary puts on a red jacket and they take a quarter each down some stairs to a garage with a basketball hoop over the door and lay the quarters on spare tires. Junior returns for the last quarter.

Meat looks bloody. And dirty. Man, d'you drag it behind the truck? You run it down first?

Junior: It's good meat, Gary. Anyway, look, let's settle up. I need some birch. Got a load of birch?

In the yard. Dont take my dry stuff.

We want lengths.

Lots of lengths.

Okay, Gabe. Move over.

Gary pulls down the door and doesnt even look at them. The yard next door. A heap of stacked eight-foot lengths of birch.

Junior: We're late, but this is good wood. Take the dry stuff. They take over a cord.

Gabriel packs for the airport. He has a cheap flight back. He's stacked frozen cuts from last year's moose in a cardboard box padded with newspaper. Another box has pickled onions, pickled beets, mustard pickles and tomato chutney.

Mom: Got room for spuds?

In the basement in a barrel of sawdust are the blue potatoes. He fishes out about forty pounds.

When I was going grey, I told your Dad he wouldnt love me any more. He got upset. Which means he must've thought it a little. Anyway I've written you all a little something and for your Dad I've said, if we both make it, look for someone with red hair.

She says, I won't be hovering in heaven, as some people claim. And if you win an Academy Award dont say you know your mother's watching. I won't know anything until the resurrection.

Seeing him off. Junior: You should buy my Dart, Gabe. Go back in the Dart. I'd have to take the stock car mirror off though, I want that. Parts are dirt cheap. Only problem is it's rear wheel drive, so you got to have weight in back in winter on those hills in town.

But he wants five hundred for it.

Dad, sizing up the wood. So where'd you go for that?

Junior: In off Georgetown Road.

See Anthony?

No. No one in there.

Funny you didnt see Anthony. On a Sunday.

We were in a little further along, hey Gabe.

Gabriel nods.

It's good yellow birch. You didnt have trouble with the saw. It cuts good.

I've found it losing power.

I was gonna tell you about that, Dad. I can have a look at it before I go.

I'd appreciate that, June.

And Gabriel shakes hands with Junior. Then hugs his mother, who's come down. It's good to have you, she says.

It's on their way to the airport. His father says, I hate to guess what you two were up to this morning.

Pause.

All I know is. That wood wasnt cut today.

But he helps Gabriel with the potatoes and shakes his hand at Departures. He hands him a piece of wood. Written on it with today's date is,

I, Al English, gave to my son Gabriel, a quantity of moose meat. Tags #02946. He will be transporting said moose to St John's where he lives.

The woman swipes his feet. Steel toes, she says.

Are they?

She nods.

When the boxes go through she halts the conveyor. She scrutinizes the x-ray. You got moose steaks in there?

Yes.

Lucky you, she says. And hits the switch.

Gabriel sees his father waiting behind the glass; he mouths something but Gabe can't understand it. He nods anyway. His father now in pantomime, and he sees it: the police coming to arrest Gabe. His father encouraging, and they both know he could have been angry.

Two weeks later, in a letter from his mother:

Your Dad said there was a smell coming from the back of the truck. He says he found a second heart.

Let's Shake Hands Like the French

I ran there in the dark and rain. I had just started running. It's a public acknowledgement of fitness. People were saying, Hi Gabe, saw you running.

The rain had melted most of the snow, but there were still humps on the sidewalks from shovelled driveways. In a garden two patches of ice melting to form a white question mark. I ran through an unfamiliar part of St John's: Tom Brennan's Hairstylist had red and gold bars of wallpaper, a lustre of stained glass. There was a green Jesus glowing from a plexiglas booth outside St Patrick's. The church had grey turrets that looked, in the rain, like plasticine.

I had time to admit that I was reluctant to meet Eric. This was a new year, and one resolution had been to confess to true feeling. It was exhilarating to chant aloud, as I ran, *I'd rather not see him.* By voicing it, I made meeting Eric into a form of choice, a willing realization that I was, if nothing else, alive. It is akin, I suspect, to a person considering his options and deciding, I'll pretend I *have* killed myself. Then you can shed obligation and unravel despair from your throat. The rest of life is a bonus, ta-da. This logic, unfortunately, is of no solace to the truly depressed. I had inherited my mother's buoyant optimism.

Eric Peach had dyed his hair black, and he hadnt forgotten his eyebrows. The fact that his eyebrows were dyed made it a more careful decision, a decision based on a mixture of craziness and vanity. He wasnt wearing glasses and there was a cigarette burn between his eyes. He wore an immense charcoal blazer. He had a big frame now.

I pointed him out to the nurse, I'm to see Eric Peach.

Gabriel English.

He liked saying my full name. It sounded respectful to him, and it honoured him that a man with such a name was coming to visit him. Or, he wanted to show that he had equivalent manners. He assumed I was a gentleman.

We shook hands and I followed him down a corridor to his room.

He said, You can spot my room from afar because the tiles change colour at the door. He said, with key in lock, The tiles anticipate the suite. He laughed and then he tried to keep the laugh to himself. I remembered then how nettled he'd get when a textbook said the paintings of Braque anticipated a

such-and-such in German politics. He despised the word cul-
mination too. Words that alluded to an insight that never
existed. He hated how the idea of evolution had garnered an
air of intentionality around it, as if species were thrusting
themselves forwards on purpose. His mouth would turn bitter
at these soft, confidently written, published sentences.

I got a window and my own bathroom.

Bathroom's big.

When they gave me the spot first time? I said where's the
bathroom because I need to be close to one and the orderly
said There it is. Mine's the only room that got one.

He tilted his head to see if this had meaning. Eric was
always checking what had just been said for importance, eaves-
dropping on his own conversations.

I hung my running jacket in amongst his shirts. There were
no chairs so we both sat on the bed. We sat there, our feet
almost touching off the edge of the bed, which made us both
tight, and then he got up and lifted a pair of sneakers, a stack
of CDs and two cans of Pepsi off the chest of drawers and sat
on top.

I got one for you.

He handed me a Pepsi. I hadnt had a soft drink in about
three years.

There was a small bloodstain on his pillow.

Two B North is the best floor in the hospital, he says. They
said, Where you want to go? and I said, I want to be north.
They said, Where? and I said, To be north. Two. B. North.

He had to get a light. He hid the cigarette under his sleeve.

Youre not supposed to smoke in the rooms, see.

He opened the door quietly, just enough to slip through.

I sat and drank the soft drink and picked up a David Bowie CD and when Eric returned with lit cigarette I nodded, wagged the CD to let him know that I remembered it, that he had given me this very album; but this fact made him stiff as it suggested how little he'd moved on since university. He had been studying piano back then, and I'd met him on the sidewalk near the laundromat shared by the residences. The left side of his moustache was stained with nicotine and a lens in his glasses was cured yellow. He had no coat even though it was near zero, and he professed to be inured to cold, that people were too obsessed with keeping warm. I sat down on the curb with him. There was a rawness coming out of his bent elbows and knees.

I've never been comfortable with material comforts. Or, I've not felt worthy of the goods and services available. Not guilty, but responsible in a vague, collective way for the massive wrongs that are done in the world to protect my standard of living. Eric was slipping off this grade and I wanted to watch him; he was my sole contact with, for lack of a better word, the oppressed. Meanwhile I shared a cement-block third-floor apartment with three other undergrads, where, for lunch, we split a tin of tuna (stretched into four sandwiches), and a can of condensed pea soup — young, ironic men destined to take their positions in the global frenzy of turning a buck. Our university newspaper's logo was a tender panda with FIGHT THE OPPRESSOR encircling it. That was me, snared by my silent acceptance of a stealthy coercion into the soup of cause and effect that explicitly governed the world's wealth, with no real feeling of remorse or sin on my part. Through no fault of my own, I would enlist into this spirit of commerce. I was agreeable, talented and a conformist. Eric: gifted, disruptive, ungrateful. He had been kicked out of university residence for setting fire to his room. His long hair had been singed by it. He said he'd placed two batteries together and then wrapped steel wool around the polarities, just like his father used to do in the woods. Flame had sputtered out and caught the curtain.

Eric spilled some Pepsi in the heel of one sneaker and tapped the ash in.

I smashed my glasses in the lock-up, Gabe. I did myself some bad in there.

You look good. You look handsome.

Go way.

You do. Without the glasses. And the hair suits you. That jacket is huge.

I've got small arms, though.

He asked after Doris, was reassured when I said we were still together. Doris had always been friendly to him and I suspected he might make a play for her if ever we broke up, just because I know few people were ever kind to him. This was not anything I ever mentioned to Doris.

He had been to Toronto for eight weeks and three days. The fleshpots of Upper Canada, to use Smallwood's expression — Eric was from Gambo too, and knew all about our Father of Confederation. The best and the brightest young New-foundlanders, laying juteback carpet and laying nothing else, Eric said, for ten dollars an hour. He'd met a woman named Anne. Anne with an E. He knew this because he'd asked her. She's pretty, with short hair.

Eric Peach was speaking of Anne-with-an-E as if she were still present, and might still be conscious of him, concerned for his welfare; he needed to equal Doris, to let me know he was okay on that score, even though he would joke about the fact he was a twenty-six-year-old virgin.

I met Anne in a bar and said, Can I buy you a beer? and she said, no and I asked if she wanted to dance and she said no and then I met her in the café and, You want a coffee? She said no and I said, Can I sit here? and she said, I guess I can't stop you and then I asked her name and she told me and all about the E and then she left.

Then you came back.

They said I had a bomb on board. I didnt have no bomb and I was telling them that and they were getting all hysterical.

Who.

The people on board Flight 826 to Halifax and St John's — they kept accusing me and it was ridiculous and they landed in Deer Lake, emergency landing, and I was placed into the gentle custody of our True North Strong and they drove me to the Clarenville lock-up.

He tossed the cigarette in the toilet bowl and flushed it. He said, I guess you got to go now.

I asked him how long he thought he was in for. He said the

results of a psychiatric evaluation would take a couple of weeks and then it was up to him.

He said, Let's shake like Rimbaud and Verlaine.

And we shook hands, looking away, as we'd learned from the French.

I didnt see Eric for another three years. Every few months I'd receive a letter, usually forwarded, typed in all caps on a manual typewriter, the kind with a spool of worn red-and-black ribbon, which made the letters appear half in red, as if his meaning was in flux. The letters grew shorter, and repetitive, as if he'd suddenly lost interest in the exercise and was merely keeping in touch: *Still* in Gambo, living with my parents. I drive in to Clarenville every three weeks for a lithium injection.

He'd offer a line on how hard it is to give up smoking, that he heard they add fibreglass to the tobacco. He had gone three weeks now without a beer. He listed off the new books at the Gambo library (Ayn Rand and Julian Barnes) and then, abruptly, said that he should go, he supposed. His signature was large and always in the blue ink of a simple Bic. Sometimes a hasty, startling poem added to the bottom: I am dogs pounding each other dispassionately. I am dogs locked at the cock and cunt. His stamps were either the Queen or the flag, nothing fancy. Often the letters were torn down with a ruler as if he was saving paper.

Then I met him in Avondale.

This was after my brother had died and I was sometimes

staying out at Helen's. I was encouraging her to take long weekends or a time out in the summer. I looked after Martin and he educated me in the mothering of goat, chickens and rabbits. Martin knew the names of wildflowers and insects. He liked me because I resembled his father and I was noticing bits of Bruce in him. I had never thought I was much like Bruce. Martin had the English gene for long legs, but the rest of him took after Helen.

I had broken up with Doris, and split with Femke (both of whom Martin had met and liked) and begun courting Lydia. Martin was impressed with her. They had met a few times, when Lydia visited from Montreal. She was still living there and I had sent her, to this point, eighty-three letters. I was averaging a letter every thirty-six hours. Helen had warned me against infatuation. I said, how do you know youre infatuated. She said, when your work suffers.

I realized that, at twenty-nine, I was still unmarried, had never lived with anyone (except roommates, for financial reasons). I didnt own a house, was still ignoring a hefty student loan, had no real job, or prospects, was not accumulating RRSPs. But I was taking care of my teeth, the fridge was stocked with my favourite foods, I went to all the movies and enjoyed buying swanky clothes and furniture second-hand. I owned a money toilet — a ten-year-old Toyota Tercel. I was living the same way I had in university and I understood this was due to my lack of commitment to the world. I couldnt buy in. I was stalled, dumbfounded by the idea of grasping an ideology. I never held an argument from a principled position the way some of my friends did. I couldnt be reliable or predictable (at least I didnt think so). Every instance seemed to be that, a particular instant, judged by its own merits, never compared. If someone said, What do you think of abortion? I said, Which abortion are you talking about? Refusing to compare meant I lacked a bank of experience to judge events by, and I knew this was a ridiculous way to run a life, but I could not abandon it for the generalizing of moments, the ranking, that was required if you adopted a philosophy. I was astonished at the depth of some people's convictions, and I confessed to undisciplined, naïve views.

That's why I loved hanging out with Martin. Most children are willing to think anything. They are brimming with What-ifs. I was coldly aware, though, that in the company of Martin, I wasnt fulfilling who I was; instead I was an assistant to someone else's world, replacing his father, or Helen. I could hear a small, whiny voice: When will I be me.

I should state that there are moments I've had with Martin that have shaped me. We were fishing, once, in the pond close to Helen's house, just after Bruce had died. I was coaxing Martin's line out to a known trout, and it snapped his dry fly. At that moment a shooting star flared, banked slowly in front of us, and vanished in a sky that was more blue than black. Martin stared at me with this double luck, a moment he hasnt forgotten even though it happened half his lifetime ago.

I had the Tercel, and I would drive out to Avondale, where Helen and Martin lived. I had a desiccated gyrfalcon's claw dangling from the rear-view mirror. Martin and I discovered the claw on the stone beach, tangled in a gill net laid out to dry. The claw looked vicious in its protracted clutch. The bird had seen a fish in the net, had plunged from a thousand metres, had been caught. Years later I found out what a tercel was — a male hawk. Martin was fascinated by the claw. It dangled like some pre-historic child's mobile.

I had time to think during those drives. Sometimes I'd look at myself through Martin's eyes. He had seen me with three quite different women. I wondered what that meant to him, my instability, my uncommitted life. It seemed he easily danced from the idea of Doris, to Femke and then over to Lydia. He did not resent the loss of a person, as long as I replaced that person with someone equally nice. It was true that all three women loved Martin.

It was also true that, during these new full-blooded months of wooing Lydia, I wasnt much good to anyone. I was brooding, stunned in love, and not working. I had halted work on the novel; instead I was writing Lydia. I was thinking, even in the frenzy of my yearning, in a ruthless way: that I could use the stuff I was sending her. Cannibalize it for the novel. I kept photocopies. I was admiring the passion in my writing, but I had cultivated the professional distance to recognize that the intimacy in the passion would only be embarrassing, especially to Lydia, if made public. I'm harder to embarrass — a fact that Lydia jots down in the drawback column of going out with Gabriel English. But I knew that embarrassment was not the emotion a reader wanted to feel.

As I drove out to take care of Martin I skipped through the facts: Helen is on a week-long watercolour retreat in the Wilderness Area, with three other women in two canoes. I am to pick up Martin from the bus stop a little after three. There are notes on the kitchen table about how to take care of the animals, make sure Amanda visits, a cell phone number for Helen.

I waited in the car for the school bus. I thought, now there's something you can rely on, the shape and colour of a school bus. I watched it spit out Martin, small and seriously engaged in lugging his school bag on his shoulder.

I asked Martin what he wanted for supper and he began to censor his thought. He was a sensitive kid. He knew what was in the fridge. What was that, I said. What did you just think.

Pizza.

We drove to Sal's Pizza. We ate slices sitting on the warm hood of the Tercel. I had decided anything Martin wanted to do we'd do. I was happy here. When you have a child temporarily in your charge, life has immediate, obvious meaning. A base obligation can be a relief.

Martin was dutiful and obedient. Helen was raising him polite and mannered, which is refreshing to see in a boy. He brushed his teeth and chose two stories for me to read. He requested the bedroom door be left ajar. A wedge of hall light lay over his chest and chin. I knew how important it was not to feel cut off from the world as youre drifting asleep. The soap was wet and I knew he'd washed his face. Martin told me all the rules that had built up around him and the house. I could rely on him to be thorough with routine. We were both glad there were rules to go by.

I scanned the bookshelf and began reading a biography of Gwen John.

It was after midnight when the screen door opened without a knock. It released a hollow crack like a dropped icicle. There was a hand, then a man in the dark who looked comfortable with the porch, who knew his way around.

Oh hi. Helen here?

No.

You her husband?

For a moment I considered being her husband. I said, I'm Gabriel.

Then I could see it was Eric. And he could see it was me.

Well, well, Mr English.

His cheekbones were swollen around the eye sockets. As if he was wearing a small pair of spectacles under the skin. His hair was cut short, in thick blunt wedges. He swung the edge of the door a little between his fingers.

I tried calling you a few times, he said, but there was no listing for a Gabriel English. Or even a G. English.

I said that I was leery of being in the book. That I didnt even have a credit card. That I used false names to order magazines, just so I'd know who *Harper's* had sold my name to.

And what do you do with that information?

I confessed I did nothing with it.

Just peace of mind, I guess, he says.

I explained I'd moved a few times, had travelled, had lost touch. Eric, gratefully, left the remainder unsaid (which was, that he'd been in Gambo the whole time and I could have reached him easily enough).

He said all last winter he shovelled Helen's driveway. He felt like Ho Chi Minh, he said. Ho had shovelled snow one winter in black Harlem.

I said that was a bizarre fact. And didnt believe him.

Again, that laugh. As if he's uncertain what he's said is funny. He touches the cold woodstove.

He said he was now a resident at Glory Path, a Home for retards, as he called it. The Home was just up from Helen's. I knew this, as there's a sign at the bottom of the road. Eric had been there about eight months.

He said, I just come over to use Helen's phone. I think I've electrified the Home.

He described how he'd been nailing up a picture in his room but it kept slipping crooked. He'd laid the picture on the bathroom floor and it slid along and slapped up against the baseboard like something out of *The Exorcist*. What, I say. What?

The nail. I think I hit some wires.

Eric Peach remains in the shadow of the porch door because the kitchen lightbulb is too strong. He is allergic to artificial light, and light reacts violently to him. He says he would appreciate my telephoning the electrician who had wired Glory Path.

Eric gives me the name — Matty Tucker — and his number. When I have Matty on I hand over the phone.

Eric relates the story to Matty. He catches my eye and points to the lamp by the phone. It had begun to flicker wildly. I turn it off. I hear him say, So, Matty, you replaced Judas? They chose you over Barsabas?

He listens to Matty's response and then hangs up. His hand still holding on to the receiver. He is a dark form quietly deciding something.

Well, Matty thinks it's just a magnetic thing. That I should go to bed out of it.

The freezer begins to click and Eric Peach says, That's giving off static electricity because of me.

The freezer emits an entirely foreign groan.

He says, I guess the youngster's in bed.

This makes me a little uncomfortable. Yes, I say.

Martin, he says. Helen gone long?

A week. She left today. (I am a man who gives out little information.)

He asks me to turn off the outside porch light and I realize he's leaving.

He excuses himself and, with each step, says Fuck. Fuck. Fuck. Back to Glory Path.

The freezer stops clicking.

I knew that Helen visited the Home, she brought goat's milk to some of the residents, as the staff calls them, and some of the residents wandered up the driveway and played with her meal rabbits. I know that Bruce tended to avoid them and, with him gone, they were coming over more often, and further up the driveway. Sometimes they sat on the old bus seat on the porch. Martin told me this.

I fall asleep jockeying through this reminder of how small life is under Newfoundland's big ear, that Eric would be here, of all places. In the morning the stairs alert me. Martin is trying to sneak up on me. The careful, slow creak indicates stealth, a trait I have. He wakes me by playing finger shadows across the sun in my face. I realize light has a weight to it, pressing on me, which his fingers relieve.

Last time I used the flat end of a nail, remember? I stroked it over your foot.

No, I say. I dont remember.

Last time when you were giving Mommy a break.

It's only 6:13 on the clock radio.

Get in, I say.

No. I'm hungry.

I ask him what he wants and he says, What is there.

There's cereal.

Pause.

I said there's cereal.

If I dont answer that means I dont want it.

There's a boiled egg.

There's toast.

There's a glass of blood.

No there's not.

Well.

An orange.

Three ginger hens have spent the night roosting in a spruce near the goat. They look large and ridiculous in the tree, but they wear an expression that says, We are wild chickens, do not laugh at us. The goat's head is tilted in the small cut-out window, waiting.

Martin crouches into the henhouse. With his eyes closed he feels for an egg. And out of the white hay is an egg. Voilà, he says.

Martin says the kids all sit on the bus with their knees together, lunch boxes on their laps. And they twiddle the handles, like this.

He asks if he can watch me shave.

He says, Wipe your lips now.

He sits on the toilet seat, mesmerized.

Where's the button to push down on? That's an eraser. That's what I'm calling it — it erases your skin. Wipe off your mouth now, that makes you like a clown.

He says, I used to watch Daddy shave. When he didnt have a beard.

I drive Martin down to the bus stop. The brakes are spongy and the car slides a little on the gravel. But we make the bus.

There's Amanda.

Amanda waits for him. She's a girl four years older than him. She's the daughter of the mortician and she has described to me the various stages of preparing a body. I remember being shocked that someone so young should have witnessed a vacuum sucking out bodily liquids, and chemicals injected into the head. Martin clicks out of his seat belt. Amanda stares at me through the windshield. I see her mouth ask Martin a question about me. The yellow door snapping shut and he's gone.

I make the turn gently, for the steering is shot. The deep, cold brook, and the juniper turning. I know I'm going back to bed.

I dream of Lydia. She approaches me and asks, Are you interested? And I say I am. But she is thinking I am Geoff Doyle, and Geoff appears and I have to tell her I'm not Geoff. Geoff is someone I knew in high school. He's a dispatcher now at the taxi stand on Caribou Road. Geoff has two kids and, the last time I saw him, he giggled at the astonishment of his predicament.

On Saturday we walk to the shooting star pond. I ask Martin to identify a field of dead, curled shafts. He frowns, then finds one strand that still has maroon sprigs. Fireweed, he says. In the book, he says, all the flowers are alive. They dont have pictures of them dead.

We fight in the afternoon. He wants me to call Amanda.

I'll call Amanda to the phone, but you have to ask her up.

No, you ask her.

I'm not asking her.

Ask her, he implores. Ask her ask her.

I say, Sometimes youre a pain in the arse.

He quietens, holds his breath for a moment.

I'm sorry, I say. Martin.

A huge cry blurts out. It astonishes both of us.

You hurt my feelings, he says.

I reach a hand to him.

No.

He goes upstairs. Through the banister rungs he says, I want to be depressed for ten minutes.

When Amanda speaks she leans from her chair, she makes this movement with her hands between her knees, one hand palm up, the other down, with fingers clawed. She's a great story-teller.

Martin tries hard to emulate Amanda. He changes his opinion to coincide with hers. Amanda doesnt like the colour red, and Martin wavers, but decides to risk his feelings. I like red, he confesses. They sleep upstairs, at midnight, after a movie. They wanted to make a bed by me, but I said I'd sleep in the spare room.

I make pancakes for them and Amanda says, Theyre thin. Martin: Theyre flatter than a pancake. Amanda laughs at that. Flatter than a pancake, she says. That's a good one.

It's then we see Eric Peach out the living room window, leaning against the woodhorse. Amanda and Martin make googly eyes.

Eric and I follow the brook down to the road. We sit on a damp wooden bench beneath a loud willow. A fire truck screams by, slows and brakes by a house not far from the funeral home. Nothing newer than a fire truck, Eric says. He is wearing a crisp jean jacket — all his clothes seem new, or carefully laundered. I notice, in the natural light, that his face is bloated and pasty, as if he'd eaten a year's worth of deep-fried food.

We watch the polished truck reverse and manoeuvre towards a hydrant. I ask Eric about the lithium. He says it's hard to be certain, but he feels his mind is slower on it. He agrees with the doctors that it makes him reasonable. He knows his tendencies. How do I seem to you?

Frustrated, but resigned to it.

He nods a long time at this.

I felt then that I was losing Eric, like a lost packet of letters over the side of a ship. He was a man I hardly knew now, had connected to once, briefly, but now recognized by appearance only; and even that had altered. I knew too that there was no one else like me in his world. A wind was blowing on him that had been unmolested for thousands of miles. A hot desert wind.

We notice a woman open a window in the smouldering house. She leans her fat forearms on the sill. She speaks calmly to her friend across the road, who is standing at her screen door. She smiles, as people often do in the face of personal tragedy. They are taking a heavy stretcher out of the house — they tilt the body through the porch like furniture. I see Amanda hammering a parade xylophone on her garden — silver curls around golden bars; and Martin is tossing a bicycle tire over cold telephone wires. They are both watching the spectacle. The shadow of a wire slaps black on the wire next to it. The wires moor the houses to the street. The woman's short white hands disappear as the firemen come to rescue her.

Eric rubs his forehead. He says the world must be a very dark and cold place for fire. Sometimes the heat of a memory is a forest fire in the distance. Gambo, he says, is always threatened by fire. Nothing worse than a hot wind. A fire with its light gone out. A fire with low self-esteem.

He said the day the residence was gutted he saw a woman testing a clothes iron at a yard sale. She was melting a mound of snow with it. She made a flat surface. Now why should I remember that? What's the point of that?

His hand is pressed so hard to his forehead that, when he releases, I can see the impression of eyebrows on the tips of his fingers.

We are outside the city's protection, he says. Wild dogs hunt caribou in those woods. Dogs can drag a caribou down by gripping the snout and suffocating it. This happens in Gambo, he says. All the time.

He stretches his eyes, as if through the sockets he can relieve the pressure of a massive headache. I should go, I suppose.

He clasps his knees and stands. We shake hands, looking away, but I betray our pact and watch him slope off down the road, his knees slightly bent. He has a funny gait. Amanda and Martin come running past him, and Amanda is mimicking Eric's walk now. Martin says, That's just like him. And I laugh and then feel bad.

Amanda: My Dad he dont like Eric Peach. He thinks if you hang around with simple people, you turn simple yourself.

I can see Martin agrees with this, either because he's affecting an amiable presence to win Amanda's consideration, or, through his own self-sculpting sense of right and wrong, he's judged Eric too.

Diaphanous Is a
Good Word for You

Felix walks us to the car in his slippers.

The further you walk with those departing, Lydia says, the more you like them.

We drive up the white hill to Lydia's. She is singing the song of wanting. The road unused since a new, soft snow. The car hushed. One line is: Every time I remember, I try to forget.

You should record that with just the car going through snow.

Lydia: Diaphanous is a good word for you.

I park with the tires tight to the curb. She searches for a house key. She rummages in her purse, holding it up to her nose, as if light will come from her eyes. The rough zipper. She is always banging her head.

Hi, I say.

Oh, hi! she says.

And we pretend we're not going out. We're careful where we lay our eyes. It's a strong flirtation.

I say, If I had a key you wouldnt have to look.

She says, I guess I prefer to look.

We take off our shoes in the porch, the first time since last winter.

As we undress there's light banking off a low pressure over the Atlantic. She pulls the drapes and says, I love drapes.

A square brim of morning leaks around the drapes. I say, A boxing ring is a square.

She nuzzles into my back. She doesnt like the small high windows out in Heart's Desire. You should be able to sit at your kitchen table, she has said, and see someone coming to your front door. And your idea of a door on the corner of a house — I think subtlety should be left to art.

The man I rent from was in the war. He built the windows high because he was afraid the Japanese would invade Trinity Bay. He wanted to have a cup of tea and not get shot.

When she asked why couldnt I have any vices, be prone to depression, she said it half seriously. She was looking at me and I know she was comparing me. There's something too safe about me.

She had written LET'S GO on my pants. And I had said to Felix Griffin, We have to go. Her glasses lifted on her cheeks. In the car: My back was killing me on those chairs. Do you know — she bangs one closed fist on top of the other — what this means?

You told me in Montreal.

So what was it with all those photographs of you in the arms of old girlfriends? And what did Marguerite mean when she asked if we were seeing each other then?

When I had you over for supper that first time, when Marguerite was pregnant.

And we were just dating.

I was wooing. In fact, I had been seeing you, but you werent seeing me.

Lydia: But Marguerite said, I want to hear it from Lydia. Sounded like you might have been sleeping with someone in September.

Well, I wasnt.

Lydia is quiet with this.

It wouldnt matter, I say, except why didnt I tell you?

Yes.

Marguerite Griffin, speaking into her left elbow. Eating pizza and she'd said to Lydia, You could do with TM. You have some tension. Youre close to your parents. You take care of them. Youre ready to have kids but he doesnt seem to be. Maybe five years. She says to me: You might need TM ten years from now, when you have two kids. Smiling. She says, You might get frustrated at serving people.

Marguerite's teeth. She had a molar extracted and since then her mouth has drifted to fill the space. Her wedding smile won a contest, Felix says. The gap between her front teeth dragged to the side.

Lydia had pushed an empty glass into a ring of spilled beer.

She'd said, Can't you have any vices? Drink too much? Be prone to depression? While Marguerite and Felix Griffin spoke of their son, turning the leaves of photo albums, of growing old and watching your child look at you as you both lie on the bed. Lydia: What is young? Felix: A Viennese psychologist.

It's good to see you guys it's so great it's . . .

And he walks us to the car.

That bit about the small high windows. That I'd choose to live in a house like that. The things I live with that Lydia wouldnt. But this criticism always comes when she gets very close to me. As if she'll sit on my lap, think about sharing a house, and then have one last good look. Lydia will sit down and say, I love drapes. And if I say theyre a dam against the light, she'll consider it and agree. That's what she means by diaphanous, and sometimes she admires it.

A fine ash of snow. Lydia out for a run. I know this because her sneakers are not in the porch. Snow on all the cars as I make coffee, one hood free of it, a warm motor. Snow connects. All the warm days contract as last Christmas hurtles forward. It's not returning in time, it's having time rush into the future at you, until all that's left of summer is one warm motor.

Lydia's face that night, the tip of her nose flattened on a storm window, looking in until Felix spots her. The light of the lamp on her face. When I lived with Felix and Marguerite. Felix moves his knight and laughs, Your baby's home. I run out with my slippers on, bowl her over in the ploughed driveway.

Merry Christmas. How long have you been watching? Oh, she says, I've been watching you a long time.

I plunge the bodum and get a pan boiling for poached eggs. I pour in a dribble of vinegar to keep the eggs together. Lydia jogging to a walk up the road, cooling down. She checks every driver, to recognize them and wave. Sometimes, if they roll down the window, she'll lean in and chat.

I slice bread for toast.

Good morning, she says.

Stranger, I say.

My period just started.

Her hair held back in a pink sweatband, her face red and fierce. Her face. It has a tight look of excitement you see in mummies, that drawn skin, as if the moment of death was intense. Her clothes are hot, moist from melted snow and sweat. Dont touch me, she says.

Do you know the exact moment?

It's a wetness. No baby this month. She smiles, her small teeth rows of white corn. I'll just have one egg, she says.

Do you want to have a baby?

Sometimes.

We eat and then I load up the car. I tell her the Griffins are driving in Monday.

I'll try and come, she says.

We kiss at the door and she realizes I'm really going. She says, I dont want you to leave now.

You'll be glad when I'm gone.

It's not that I'll be glad.

It's that you live with what's around you.

And this is partly true. But I didnt state it as a strength. She'd said that thing about no baby. That was a statement of commitment.

She says, Your living out there is a bad idea. But, she says, who can say theyre writing a novel from Heart's Desire?

Lydia, all advice for the proper act, if only I'd listen. I once saw her advise a woman on her signature. I am by genes a stubborn man. I govern my own acts. Lydia would say I am defiant. She thinks I dont feel guilty, but I do feel guilty, although it's true I'm not Catholic.

If youre not Catholic and youre from Corner Brook youre doomed you are a loser a big fat zero you have all that against you and you werent even born here! is what her brain thinks during an impasse.

I turn on the radio, blast the heat, and head for the crosstown arterial. I love the power of the amp in my little Honda. The heavy speakers. The defrost still delicately melting the rear window after eleven years. And now a clear Bulgarian choir fills the car. Felix says he took singing lessons in his thirties. He'd been working in a fabric plant in Kingston. There was a forty-mile drive in the morning when he'd leave his first wife and two daughters, enter a bedroom community, then hit the 401. I think of Felix as I shift into fifth. He would tune the car radio to 96.3 and sing late fifties hits. The plant was in an industrial park carved out of Canadian shield. He wore earplugs in the plant. He was in charge of the hardening process, where oil is superheated then spun out and chilled into fibre. He would sing over the whirling spools. He tells us these things because I ask him and I can see Marguerite has not heard this particular story of his previous life. He sings Tosca as he changes their boy in my old bedroom. Felix envies Lydia her singing life, that she can make a go of it.

There is a moose on the highway. A cow, skittering down the wet road to the Tilton turnoff. I follow. It stares at me from the slush, tall like a camel, waiting, patient. Then a grown calf emerges from the woods, they talk for a moment, catch up, and trot off together behind a corrugated building. I stop into a Foodland and find red peppers at a dollar ninety a pound.

In a hundred minutes I am in Heart's Desire. Flakes of frost driving in hard through the dashboard air vent.

Cory Langer pedals over with Gerard and David St George. Braking on ice. Very polite, well behaved. Standing over their bikes, watching me pour in antifreeze.

Cory: I got some moose steaks for you, Gabe.

He's roped them into a wooden fruit crate over his back wheel. Plastic-wrapped, frozen, on styrofoam trays.

Thank you, Cory.

Lydia in?

I left her in town.

We was up to the mall, Gabe, looking for bearings.

What do you want with bearings?

For our slingshots. For shootin birds.

There's a mall?

Laughter.

It's what we calls it. The dump. We calls it the mall cause you can get everything you wants up there.

They found a wooden bead braid and they are using the beads as practice ammo.

Gerard: I could take out that window cross the road.

They say the mall is up by The Gannets and in fall I can get berries on the track behind Fonse's and that guy Matt across the road has a hole in his toolbox so he can sneak a gun into the woods after the season and he beat his wife and went to jail for it and you got a good car dont ever buy a Ford like what we got.

We are talking about snaring rabbits and I say do you have beagles, and Gerard says what's a beagle and Cory pushes his front wheel a little in the snow and, looking into the bare alders, says, A beagle is a rabbit dog, Gerard.

On the phone to Lydia: Theyre best friends, from the way he said that. They want me to go to church tonight.

Lydia: I'll sing you a song when youre in church. I'll think of you genuflecting.

And what's that padded shelf for, in the pew.

You bend your knees.

But I've got bad knees.

Hold on to a pew. You dont have to. In fact maybe you shouldnt.

I tell her about the moose, of roasting ten red peppers. I say, Take care of your throat.

Did you see the poster?

Yes.

Wilf did that for me, she says.

Saturday in Heart's Desire. When there's no hockey in Whitbourne it's church. I meet Cory's mother, Joan Langer, who looks down at her feet to speak but meets my eye to listen. I thank her for the moose steaks and I can see she'd rather I didnt mention them. The priest boxes with Cory. He's got a good feint and weave. I hear a man say, Just across the water in Little Heart's Ease. Sally Ann man done it. He has some guts if he did.

Another man: That's what they says he done it.

To yourself.

They say.

Usually somebody knows somethin.

In a small community.

They consider Little Heart's Ease a small community. Where a priest was doused in gasoline and burned. And now there's talk of a girl and the priest and local revenge. Graffiti on the rocks beyond this church says I LOVE HEART'S DESIRE. There is no fish plant now.

In the pew, Cory: Father Mews he got a expensive car and he's a excellent man, he smokes and he wrestles with ya.

A man with an acoustic guitar leads the choir in hymn.

Cory whispers, Kneel. I see that theyre all kneeling, so I kneel. Then he whispers, Lie down.

Theyre gonna tear down this church, Cory says, which is too bad, cause it looks like a church.

They closed the school five years ago and are breaking it into a funeral home, a place of worship and a bingo hall. The kids are bussed north to Heart's Content or south to Heart's Delight, Protestant communities. Hearts and hearts. Desire a town caught in the middle, a Catholic thing.

Gerard and Cory walk me back to the Head. David's mother, Cory says, pointing his trigger mitt. She used to live in that house. Lives in the graveyard now. Madge lives cross the road in the green two-storey house, she's a nun.

Gerard: She's not.

Cory: No, but close to it.

They name every house and who lives in it. There is sneakiness, they assure me, occurring under every roof.

Lydia calls in the small hours: she saw our photograph on her fridge. She is calling to say she misses me. She wants me to come to Montreal. Jules sent her the photo and we look great. I was at a party, Gabe, at Wilf's. I'm a lustful woman. Lots of men I find cute.

She is eating a microwaved sausage and listening to her message machine.

She says, Sometimes I feel shy. Sometimes I want everyone's attention but once I have it I freeze.

The show went good at the Spur.

I ask her not to bring home any men while I live in Heart's. Young musicians who love her voice.

You mean my body, she says. It's not the young ones who want to sleep with me. There are some men saying let's just get it over with.

I say, I like a good flirt.

But youre not a lady's man, are you — you dont fall in love with women over and over.

That's not what lady's man means.

Yes it is, she says. Wilf is a lady's man and he keeps falling.

Is he falling?

Her voice, a stoned lisp. He might be.

A lady's man is someone who doesnt fall in love. It's the sport.

Well, can you see how I find him sexy?

I see his appeal.

And Barry. Sometimes when I'm stoned and I see Barry I think of him as a spiritual leader, a vegetarian in the best physical condition he can be, his glasses, his energy — yet he can party too. We were playing a game. I had them over for supper. And we stuck words on our foreheads. His was Truth and mine was Passion.

You had who over.

Wilf and Barry. And Alexandria came up with the baby.

I say, of this, that we have a dangerous understanding. That we are both attracted to others.

Yes, she says.

Maybe youre a gentleman's woman.

No, Gabe, I'm yours.

Are you alone now?

Yes, babe.

Are you going to get up for mass?

Maybe Gaby. Let me sing you a song.

She sings the song that defies regret. There is no forced rhyme and no repeated stanza.

I am stiff with apprehension. Is she alone. What were the words on foreheads. But she called. She said Wilf told her one honest thing: that he doesnt feel a part of the human race. She said his teeth are looking great — must have got some work done on them with his royalties. Teeth. I wouldnt be surprised, she said, if theyre false. Did she call from guilt. No, she called. She shares everything with you. I asked her, When are you going to come. Maybe tomorrow night? That means she won't come. Dont be a pessimist.

The poster Wilf made was simple:

> Hi
>
> I'm playing at the Spur Saturday night
>
> No cover
>
> Lydia Murphy
>
> Thanks a lot

These new sheets, we changed the sheets. Lydia searched my cupboard, said God it's been a long time since I've dealt with this. It's true, she said. And then, as we pressed the air from fresh cold sheets on the mattress, she reiterated: I love condoms.

I said, Do you think it'll be okay.

Do you have any spermicidal jelly?

No.

That's never happened to me before. Has it you?

All I can think is your fingernail was close to the condom.

But you would have felt that.

In bed, warm. Well, you might have made me pregnant.

Yes.

Later: What do you think the chances are?

Slim. But not because you werent in there. It's the wrong time of month.

Maybe we should say a prayer.

Okay, that I'm not pregnant?

Or something more positive. That whatever happens will be a good thing.

Yes, that we'll have lots of good times no matter what. That whatever happens it'll have a college education.

I have to have faith. What makes an act okay? Look for the good in it. The redeeming side. Wilf has a bad tattoo ringing his biceps. But it's not a question of her going out with Wilf. It's one bad night. Marguerite said, I think she loves you, Gabe. She moved back from Montreal and she'd been gone five years. That's a big move.

But she won't live with me.

Marguerite: But you said she's never lived with any of her boyfriends.

Well, why not marry me?

She just has a different opinion on commitment, Gabe. A spade's a spade for her. There was this guy, Gary — this was before Felix. He was obsessed with me. When he'd buy me flowers I felt like throwing them in his face. I remember him wincing when I found Felix. He said, The taste of your own tears in the back of your mouth. That kind of devotion, Gabe, leads to anguish and ruin.

Sunday night. Lydia calls at nine from a gas station at the overpass. It's foggy and dark. If I come, she says, it'll take four more hours.

The fog won't last, I say.

I'm down to sixty kilometres an hour.

The fog is only on the barrens.

I've forgotten the groceries.

Please, Lydia, please dont turn back.

A hundred minutes later I hear her catalytic converter.

I've got a dry fire that roars in the chimney. She is writing a letter to Jules on the manual typewriter. She has the typewriter on her knees. The strong fifties wallpaper behind her makes her vanish. I watch her take page three and crumple it. She opens the woodstove door and throws it in. Noticed that, did you, she says. I notice everything, I say. Oh no you dont — I get a lot by you. She turns off the overhead light and carries a lamp to bed. She has an envelope and a book.

I asked Jules for a midnight meeting in the Park — I didnt know how you'd feel about that.

I'm fine with that.

Good.

While I'm reading she asks if I know a joke.

I can't think of one.

I wish you knew jokes, she says slowly. I like hearing jokes. Sometimes I think you'd like to laugh more.

Yes.

I help her decorate the envelope. I can smell cocoa butter on her hands.

Me: Did you have that in Montreal?

Yes. I just found it.

You were wearing it when we picked strawberries on that farm.

Craig's farm. I wasnt wearing it. I put some on. You dont wear moisturizer.

You were choosing a chicken for supper. You were bent over to watch Craig slit the throat.

Sometimes, she says, it's as if I dont know the repercussions of things. I was absorbed in how he grabbed the chicken with one thumb, how he folded it under his foot. The slender sharpened knife. And then the line of blood across the feathers and dirt. I knew it was coming and yet I didnt expect it.

I remember now. Lydia used to walk the rising streets of Montreal with Jules. They'd meet near the mountain after a movie, or if Jules had a computer class he might call and they'd have a beer with Craig. Jules might have a goatee or he might have a new prescription in antique glasses he'd stolen from a museum. Craig would drive away on his bicycle and Jules and Lydia would follow curved paths through dormant flower gardens. They watched a man duck under a bush with a blue sleeping bag.

Lydia wanted something from Jules, but he never approached her. Finally, after nine months, he said: Maybe we can kiss. But by then she had turned him into a friend. They tried kissing, but they were uncomfortable.

We lie in bed holding hands over my head. I ask if she remembers the first moment she connected to Wilf.

Wilf Jardine?

Yes.

It was at a party she held at her apartment, after the first songs. Had all the sound crew there. Got stoned. Had an out-of-body experience. Thinks she did. Could see herself looking in the mirror. A name producer asked if she wanted him to stay. No. Persisted. Then he left. Wilf asked if she wanted him close. Yes. But then she fell asleep in the bathroom with the door locked.

That's my story of Wilf, she says.

We sleep in. The woodstove empty and cold. I twist newspaper and stack kindling, blow to rouse a flame out of the ash. Something catches. I make coffee.

She had to ask which Wilf. She doesnt think of him.

Lydia, in bed, says, Have you thought about looking for a place?

I've thought about it.

What's unsaid. I'll look if you'll live with me. An old story.

But I recoil, too, from the outside pressure. Marriage should be an internal decision, and it hardly ever is.

Almost everyone is married, she says, and has children. Or at least they have children.

Cory brings over a small, sectioned rabbit on a dinner plate. Dad skinned her for me, he says. Left the kidneys, some people dont eat em any more.

He and Gerard had checked their slips and one was straightened out. Gerard set that one, Cory says, raising his chin. He woulda been big.

He says, You wasnt up by lunchtime. Cause my parents said there was no smoke coming out of your chimley.

He knew Lydia was here because her car's out there.

I knows every licence plate in Heart's Desire. I knows yours too, Gabe.

He concentrates. ATF four three one. Alcohol, Tobacco, and Firearms.

Lydia: And?

You got a Quebec plate. *Je me souviens.*

He's brought over his language homework. Mom says I should drop over more often, so. I have to write answers using these words.

One involves describing your neighbourhood to a visitor from another planet. Cory says, I guess sir doesnt mind us to use all these sentences we learn.

What do you mean?

Well, when would we use a sentence about aliens?

He turns to Lydia: Gabe knows everything.

I say: Lydia thinks I make a lot of stuff up.

There's a difference, Lydia says, between knowing something and having an opinion.

Cory: Gabe uses words sometimes in a new way. Like that
spice cardamom, you put on the chicken, you calls it warm. Do
you eat different when youre alone?

You mean different food?

No, I means the eating part. I eats like a pig if no one's
around.

Lydia makes him a poached egg. Then Gerard knocks on
the back door. He wants an egg too. Theyve never seen them
poached.

Cory: Aint it the wrong time of day to be eating eggs?

Gerard: I never tasted butter neither. Dont it cost a lot?

Lydia: Eat some off the end of your knife.

I say, In Russian novels the peasants have nothing, but they
eat fresh eggs and they have a pound of butter on the table.

Gerard doesnt want ground pepper on his eggs. It's too
fresh, he says.

They watch Lydia grind pepper until her eggs are black.

Felix and Marguerite arrive at six-thirty. I've got two baked
chickens in cardamom and a spinach salad. Marguerite has the
baby and Felix carries the chess set and two bottles of Chilean
wine. Marguerite puts the baby down. She says it's good to get
out with Felix. Drinking separately is dangerous, it can affect
your emotions.

Felix plays Scaring the Shit out of Him. This involves
crawling around the couch, thumping the carpet, hoo hoo hah

hah, and reaching out to tickle the boy. The boy gets anxious then giggles.

Felix counters with a Nimzo-Indian. We get drunk on the wine.

I end up saying I'm very poor at naming emotions truthfully. That I can allude to things, have things said which will make it understood, but to say 'x' felt 'y' is beyond me.

Marguerite: I assumed you were capable of that.

Lydia: No, he's not. All his work is this descriptive showing. It's like he's afraid to label something or diagnose it.

I know how to act truthfully, I say, but to name that action — and I never lie, though sometimes I might withhold information. I know I'm capable of that. But I choose a moral code for my own well-being. For instance, I've told Lydia I wrote a letter to a woman who obviously likes me, and she wrote back.

Lydia: I'll write you, babe.

While he's here. Oh, that's sweet.

She's going to Montreal, I say.

For how long?

I'm coming back.

We watch Felix kiss his fingers and touch them to Marguerite's face.

You know what, Felix says. I want to die an old death.

Dont we all.

I mean, I dont want to enter, for instance, a snow grooming machine. Or eat a new bacteria.

Marguerite: He wants the death to be an ancient one.

Lydia: A good old-fashioned drowning.

Yes.

The wishbone has dried on the woodstove and we break it. Lydia gets the long half. Do I make a wish now?

Youre supposed to make your wish before you break it.

Oh. Well I got my wish.

She'd wished for the longer half.

In the morning we drive to town separately, in three cars.

Lydia packs one small suitcase and a carry-on bag. I fill three pop bottles, in case the pipes have frozen. I'm to drive her to the airport and then return to Heart's.

The house is going to be a block of ice, I say. It even looks a bit smaller in the cold.

You know, says Lydia. That kind of humour I bet Cory might like.

I quietly take Lydia to the plane. She twists the rear-view mirror to apply lipstick. You think this vain? No, I say. I love the scope of your look. Youre a fashion cougar.

We sit in a coffee shop for five minutes, Lydia wearing her mother's grey canvas coat and a black choker with white shells.

If we broke up, do you think you could be polite to me?

Lydia: I hope so. It depends on how we broke up. I mean, we've almost broken up both ways. If we were resigned to breaking up.

Me: Do you think there's a difference between oral sex and, what's the word, fornication?

Intercourse?

Yes.

Yes, there's a difference.

If I had to choose, I'd want you to have sex with a guy.

I wouldnt. Oral sex isnt sex.

I think it's more graphic than sex.

You can't get pregnant or get a disease.

But it's so conscious. It means youre really into it.

So you'd rather I slept with someone.

I'm not rathering anything. But if you told me you'd sucked a guy off. I'd find that hard to forgive. It'd mean you thought about it, you didnt just lose yourself to rapture.

Goodbye at the metal detector. Through the glass partition in duty-free, I watch her line up at the boarding gate. I concentrate to make her turn, but she doesnt look.

Cory comes over as soon as I get in.

He says, Youre some fool to be coming in on weather like this.

The dark highway, streaking snow like sparks from a chimney. The coloured wires of fuses.

Lydia in?

She's in Montreal. Just about now.

Cory pauses, and I feel like saying: She'll be back, she's just visiting a former life. But then he says, I coulda gone to Montreal — we didnt raise enough money.

I say, Look at this.

In the kitchen, the running faucet has formed a clear ice mound connecting the drain to the faucet neck. Water is streaming silently through the ice.

I left it running so the line wouldnt freeze.

Cory picks up one of the green bottles of water.

That water from town?

Yes.

How come you brung it?

In case it froze up here.

But you just said you left it running.

Well, I wasnt sure if that would be enough.

Town water. When you got the best water in the world here.

You ever taste town water?

Why would I want to.

Well, how can you compare?

He studies the clarity and takes a sip.

That's healthy, he says. I come over cause Dad's got wood. I noticed your shed's a little shy of wood and if youre gonna be having visitors. He'll sell you a thousand pieces for a hundred dollars.

I only know cords.

That's more than a cord.

Tell him to name me a price in cords.

He pauses. That's stacked in your shed and everything.

How many cords you think I need for the winter?

Cory studies the woodstove. You gonna stay it all winter?

I might.

Five. That's if you dont get birch.

He says, my sister's in from town. She wants to come over.

I say, Any sister of Cory's.

I saw a grouse back there. I was crossing your gardens and

he flew up. Big though, you could get him with a rock or a baseball.

I light the stove and find, beneath it, a tissue with a drop of cologne on it. Cory's sister brings over mustard pickles, a red bow on the lid. She introduces herself as Leish. She is wearing a black leather coat. Green eyes and black hair. She is my age. She asks what I'm writing. I say (in a vague way that would bug Lydia) that I write of life's small celebrations. I ramble on because I presume she knows very little of writing and has a good listening ear. She says her father cheated on her mother and she took her and Cory and the twins and left him for a while. It was a woman just up the shore, married, in Heart's Delight. Then she says, For years, my favourite book was *The Unbearable Lightness of Being.* Then I got pissed off with how Kundera writes his female characters.

She says, I go out with Albert — he's film crew, works in Halifax, spends half his time there. I know a lot of guys who sleep around on their girlfriends every weekend. I can't understand that. Albert slept with my best friend Kay and I forgave him. Although a year after, Kay tried to make it sound different and I didnt appreciate that. I havent spoken to her in three years.

She sits down and I put on the kettle. She says, If you dont tell right away, then I dont ever want to know. That's your burden then.

But doesnt something hidden always invite suspicion?

Suspicion's there if something's hidden or not. You can tell all and still give off a whiff of treason, and that will bring suspicion.

When I open the tea chest I find a strip of paper: Lydia loves Gabe. For some reason I remember that gold and red are Lydia's favourite colours. Lydia leaves a room wearing red silk shorts. She turns in the doorway to smile. If she knew at this moment that I was thinking of her in carnal terms.

Leish says Albert wants her to move up to Halifax. But then she'd just be a wheel, she'd have to start from scratch up. He's not artistic, he works on other people's sets, she says. Completely different to you, she says. I wouldnt be able to hurt him. He's not into conversation, that's the major difference. He's mentioned marriage but I've said I'm not ready to discuss that.

Can you imagine yourself married?

Yes. But not to Albert.

This makes my blood heavy.

She says, Mom wants you to come over for supper tonight. You know the house? She leans on the deep freeze and points to a green roof out by the Head.

I lean over her shoulder to see out the frosted window. Cory's house.

She says, I was told you had blue eyes but now I see theyre green.

We're close enough that her breath touches my face. I blink.

Lydia calls from Jules' apartment and I tell her Leish Langer has invited me over. Who's Leish? Cory's sister. How old is she? Our age. Do you like her? Yes. Do you still love me? Yes. Then that's okay, she says.

She says Jules might be getting a software contract. She says Jules really likes you. He sees youve got no bullshit. She says, I missed you on the plane. I wrote you and put it in the box at the airport but I might have forgotten to stamp it. Jules couldnt come and I bumped into Annette who I met in Cegep and so now I'm meeting her and her husband tonight at an oyster bar.

Are you going with Jules.

He's gonna meet us there. Look, babe, please dont be that way.

I can see her eyes now. Her frown, from that tone of voice.

If you were on your deathbed, I say, and allowed to see one person.

I'd choose the person I'm with, she says.

You want a person who understands you, I say. The person who understands you is often not the person youre with.

Gabe, there was a man driving and I was telling him about such and such. I got into such and such and repeated myself. I realized I was repeating myself. It's part of how I tell a story, she says. I know this bugs him. We pass the turnoff. I say, You passed the turnoff. He says, why didnt you tell me before, instead of blathering on.

When he says that, Gabe? Then I know he doesnt really understand me. I dont want this person when I'm dying. I do not want him agreeing with my death in a civil way.

Sleet rains down hard. The sleet reminds me I am inside. The ground is covered in torn leaves, mainly green, the violence of wet snow and wind. Dogberry stems in leaves of ten.

The leaves stuck to the wet door frames.

A thud at the window. And all that's left is a wet feather.

What's that? Lydia says.

A bird. It was a bird. When I look it's gone.

Four of the World's
Smallest Worlds

I have been spending time with men. I am, temporarily, not interested in women — usually my best friends have been women, which has irritated my wife. I have a weariness for love and no desire to flirt. All I want is a shared, male camaraderie. Maybe this is sexual. All I know is I'm not considering the sexual side of anyone (besides my wife). I dont know if this is a permanent condition, and this is not to say that I'm not attracted to the sensual — in fact I'm excited by the knowledge (if knowledge were a bunch of sticks, as the philosophers used to say) of how to lift the caul of sexuality off a deeper, and far more interesting, layer of sensuality. I admit, though, that I might be slightly sexually depressed, but this condition is fine by me. I'm bored with primitive desires — although I'm attracted to the wants of physical and mental exercise. These wants make me, to my surprise, a perfect social companion. And this ease I was trying to understand: is it a new stage in general male growth or a unique fork in the road of my own personal development? I was searching in the men around me. In particular, Max. I was inviting Max over for supper and found it satisfying just to talk, drink vodka from the freezer door and watch him honestly weigh (at least for the moment) past lives, give his opinion on personal decisions, debate delicately with himself as he stood at the fulcrum on small points of conscience, as we chowed down on chicken tarragon and ginger carrot soup. I'm a good cook. My wife has told me that. She said that she's always gone out with good cooks.

What happened to you? Max said. And I'd said it came down to a lack of trust with Lydia. We were saying things we didnt believe, omitting detail, and then we called each other on our misprisions and since then we've been connected.

Yes, it's true that we listen to the stories of others so they will listen to us.

Max: I met Ingrid at a folk festival in Ireland. Those things are becoming like religious events. She has two kids and she's married and lives in Copenhagen. I found all this out later. I've been a year now and three thousand miles from her. And how long have we been together? Eight days?

Max says she is very beautiful.

Well, I say, I've been with a woman every day and what happened. She took me for granted and I wasnt giving her enough rope and then we got mad and now we're some place different.

I had been with my idea of beauty (my wife, four years ago, when she was my girlfriend) and it had strained me. I have gotten beyond infatuation, which beauty can drug you on. And I have heard many stories of eight-day wonders. We all have brief encounters with the perfect companion. They are perfect because of the brevity.

Max, I think, appreciates evenings spent with me. There is never delayed embarrassment. I've noticed Max taking a second look at me. I am funny, for one thing. No one has taken me for a man with a sense of humour. (My mother sent me a letter I had written to my brother when I was ten. I used to be silly and somehow, through the past two decades, I had lost this joyful spunk.) I want to reclaim zaniness. Ambition: to overhaul reserve and reclaim zaniness. And this involves, I know instinctively, avoiding the influence of women.

But this is not true. The truth is I want to ignore sex. Any time sex raises its head I shut my eyes. It's a conscious project. This may be my time of denial.

Max, in the sauna: You are insulting someone if you say their love cannot be returned. There is the lover and the beloved. To get to your point, Gabe, there is no elasticity in trust.

So he brings in trust. Love being a very simple recipe, but hard to eat. You have to like how someone looks, I say. And you like that look because youre interested in their language. By language I mean physical presence. Language informs their look. There is a difference between presence and physical beauty, which, if you mistake the two, can lead to anguish and ruin.

Max and I were playing, weekly, forty-minute periods of racquetball at the Mews Centre. We recognized a competitive zeal and, to Max's own amazement, he felt a desire to win and a disappointment if I didnt give him a good game. He says he hates meeting aggressive people and yet here we are, tooth and nail. We talk about this in the sauna afterwards, or in his car, on our way downtown to the one snooker table we like to hone our aim on.

I've known this man for thirteen years. Max and I met in an English course in my third year. He was born a decade before me, so I expect wisdom. What was my first impression of Max? He came to my apartment once after that course, it was January and he was worn down. The summer before he had split up with a woman he'd been living with and, when asked, he said, Last year was a hell of a year. I said I never thought of years as good or bad. I was a firm believer that life was a constant progression, that a year contained the previous years you'd lived. A good year is always with you. Life accumulates and culminates, my youthful hunch (I still believe in the accumulation; however, direct cause and effect have taken a bit of a beating). Max had ended it with Anita by spray-painting rust primer over an art exhibit she was having down at the Rude Finch. I knew about this graffiti before I met Max. He said, though, that he knew her work was under glass. He was going for effect and was embarrassed with the repercussions of the act. Embarrassed but still slightly pleased with the accomplishment. He also cut off all the fruit on her tomato plants. Though he didnt mean to suggest violence. The acts werent violent (although I'd contend, as most do, that they were imbued with the threat of violence — if I were Anita I wouldnt feel perfectly safe alone in his presence. Max is undoubtedly slightly emotionally erratic and therefore a candidate for performing a grievous and regrettable act).

And so started a relationship with a man which, I am surprised to say, has lasted longer than most others, though I only see him weekly, for racquetball and snooker, and long stretches can go by where nothing too significant is passed between us except general goodwill, although we have been known to sit down, get drunk and have, in polite turns, a good cry. I know Max would put himself out for any reasonable favour I asked of him, and likewise.

And now I am living in the days of this male companionship.

If we take one particular evening last week after racquetball, when we were hoping to see slices of empty green through the blinds, but there were red balls on it and there was a rolling motion. That's poetry for you. Max opens the pistoned door and I duck in under his arm. There's a fat Ethiopian and a white grad student who take the snooker table every Tuesday night and there they were again. We were hoping for maybe an hour on it. In the corner, on a pool table, are Fabrice Richoux and Winston Porter, playing nine ball. Theyre about Max's age, or at least theyre older than me, and I should point out that Winston went out with my wife for about three years, but this was a long time ago. So we buy a bucket of beer, which is five Molson products in ice, and resign ourselves to joining them.

I like Winston Porter in that polite recognition of meeting a man no more than three times a year at various gatherings, nod to and shoot the breeze with about what's new and not too personal, or, less creatively, what's fresh in the public news, i.e., journalistic news. I can make people feel uncomfortable, a fact I'm not proud of. A few years ago (before I hooked up with Lydia and after she and Winston had parted ways) Winston gave me money from his federal department to put together an anthology of fiction. It wasnt his decision, but he issued the cheque, and it was Winston I met to discuss my end of the agreement. There was something in how he handed me the money that implied he had more to do with this than I could imagine. But I could imagine, and took his look to be a delusion of grandeur. Because of that moment I've never quite understood Lydia's attraction to him, though she hardly speaks of him. He's quiet and warm and probably has a big expertise on some arcane subject that no one ever asks him about. I would suspect it has to do with various methods of drying wood — Lydia told me once that the house they lived in was built with charred timber from the 1892 fire, which razed the downtown core in the middle of winter. This salvaged lumber was sold to the middle class, the rich bought new wood. But the smoked wood was immune to microbes and never rotted. The smoke molecule, Lydia told me, making the A-OK with her thumb and forefinger, is larger than the molecules in wallpaper. So the odour remains trapped in the walls.

I, like Lydia, can appreciate a man who offers facts like this.

All three of these men — Winston, Fabrice, Max — are

living in the wake of repercussions. I'm attracted to older men precisely because I hope to glean a wisdom, some method from their examination of hindsight; this study will make my path easier and more profitable, a frail wish.

Of these men, Winston is perhaps the happiest, and hence the least reflective. This happiness is not the successful profit from some heroic personal journey, but a genetic predisposition to a simpler life, a tolerance for monotony, and therefore a greater ease at achieving self-satisfaction. I dont consider Winston's lack of reflection a bad trait, in fact I envy it. What more can any man want than to know his limit, understand what makes him happy and realize, deep within his marrow, that in another room somewhere, not too far from here, loved ones await his return.

He is a man with a well-trimmed, perhaps tinted, beard.

I should add that he and Lydia split when she was very young, wasnt ready to settle, and seemed to despise his cozy life. Though now, I'm sure, she keeps a mental record of his accomplishments (he plays a fiddle at open mike venues) and in idle moments must wonder at the life that would have been. It was her choice to leave him although they had both done foolish, damaging things.

Winston was, in fact, clewing up for the night, going home to his family, I supposed. He has two children, and I assumed pool on a weeknight is as wild as it gets for him. But when I ask him he says no, a meeting. And this further impresses me, a deeper fold of mystery in Winston. More precisely, he says, An appointment. And suddenly I realize I am by far and away his inferior, I had been judging Winston's life in terms too simple to stand a gentle audit. I had it coming to me. What a mysterious man! I noticed he was smoking, a recreational smoker. Fabrice, too, had a pouch of Gauloise tobacco by his beer. It was a perfunctory, civil exit by Winston, leaving Fabrice in the capable and relatively fresh, more novel hands of Max and me.

And I thought, an appointment? Mere posturing?

Smokers, I believe, activate a part of the brain unreachable by us non-smokers. It is a cavity devoted to the encouragement of unpredictable connections. And the fact that Lydia had gone out with a smoker, well.

Neither I nor Max, I could tell, was really into dealing with Fabrice Richoux. Not that we have anything against Fabrice — he could have been any third party. We wanted the snooker table and the tranquillity you get with circling ninety square feet of green nap under concentrated light. It's hard for two men to talk around the girth of a snooker table. But here with Fabrice, racking up nine ball on a small table with blue cloth, winner keeps the cue ball, we had to converse. This we easily adapted to. Shortest cue sits out, and, for a moment, we leaned our blue leather tips together in some musketeer brotherhood. I had it.

Fabrice reaches for the plastic rack hanging on the brass lamps and frames the balls into a tight diamond. Slowly lifting the nose of the rack. His hair buzzed short, temples receding. There is a cat in the top of his face. Max breaks. And proceeds to pot the yellow, the blue. Fabrice sits down with me and takes a packet of cigarette papers from his shirt pocket. Crosses his legs, he has big feet. So, Gabriel, he says. What's new with you. As Max angles in on the red three.

I tell Fabrice I'm busy on a new collection and he's impressed with this. He is a painter who, we all know, showed early promise, achieved national recognition, and has since faded with full-time curatorial work, an estranged wife and child. This is not a unique progression, but nonetheless tragic, especially since he was remarkably articulate for a painter. He gave a good interview. In recent years, his wife — a musician distinguished in her own right — had left him because of this artistic failing (the rumour goes), was obsessed with a woman, has since settled into being single and a devoted mother. An amicable separation (Fabrice did his best to understand), for the sake of their son, Guy. Fabrice is still seen with Connie — they negotiated the car, have dinner together weekly, and are ruthlessly honest when it comes to Guy's welfare. This I know from the meandering stories that are overheard in this, a small town with a big ear.

There are, in fact, many stories that whirl about the lives of Fabrice and his ex-wife. Fabrice having stand-up sex in my bathroom with Angela Coombs the night I launched my first collection (Angela told me this in the days when I spent time with women). Fabrice continuing to live with Connie even when her lover moved in. Fabrice sleeping in the guest room. The woman Connie was obsessed with (Adele) lived for a time in Montreal and took a room in Lydia's apartment, and Connie flew up on several occasions to dote on Adele and write songs about her in that apartment, making several references to

Lydia. Flattering references, really. I admire Connie immensely — that she would recognize she was not in love with Fabrice because he had grown out of the world of making art. He had lost her respect. Although she can swerve into the sentimental (she loved the flapper era). You could get away with this in the twenties, or if you were in your twenties, or if the songs were very good, which they often werent.

I said to Fabrice, A couple of years ago you asked me if I was as happy as I looked. And I said yes. And this befuddled you. You had read my stories and couldnt understand how a happy man could write so well.

Fabrice studies me. He is willing to get serious and I am, again, realizing that I want to be serious. I want seriousness and yet lack the words to continue this approach. Max is waiting for Fabrice to shoot on the green four. Fabrice says, I remember that. We'll get back to that. And he shoots miserably and sits down again in a heap of long limbs. He says, Life is a series of distractions. And he raises his eyebrows to the table.

Yes, I say. You see, I'm not really that happy.

This seems to hurt Fabrice.

What I do have is a buoyancy.

Fabrice: I understand that.

But to be honest I'm thinking about leaving my wife.

He nods gravely and I know he is weighing me. I am in one scale and his past is in the other. I can tell too that his mouth has about three words in it, but no finished sentence. I say, Personally, Fabrice, I dont see what keeps you going.

He looks down the length of his body. Small moments, he

says, and he has an example ready. I was watching a cat play with a pigeon. It had torn its wing, now stalking it. Batting it. A gull swooped several times at the cat, until it slunk away behind a car. And the pigeon made its escape. That made me so happy.

A series of distractions, Max says.

Fabrice: There are no objectives. This is it. This is fun. Pool is an accumulation of approximations.

And the cat's ears perk up (his receding temples) as he raises his eyebrows.

And it's as if I have said nothing.

We rotate games until midnight. I'm sitting down between shots because my ankles hurt. I ask Max if he has a flawed body part. Max says his back. Fabrice thinks about this.

Max: Fabrice is in excellent shape, he has no aches.

I wouldnt say that, Fabrice says. And then pauses. I have this tickle in my asshole.

Pardon?

A tickle.

A hemorrhoid.

No, it's not that.

Did you say youve got a tickle in your asshole?

Yes.

From this, I can tell we are going to have a perfectly honest night with Fabrice.

After midnight we split the cost of the table and Fabrice Richoux invites us to his place. He has an apartment behind a carpet shop off Empire. I have been in the house he shared with Connie: small rooms, warm with exposed yellow beams and birch floors, the third storey an A-frame which was their bedroom. Fabrice's apartment is white, no mouldings, with a corridor. It's a place you live in while going to university.

Fabrice: Excuse me.

He takes the corridor. I'm not sure where Guy must sleep and it makes me wonder if Fabrice ever gets him. There are beer in the fridge, he says, from beyond.

Max is careful when he sits. I have seen a frailty grow in his hips. And his forehead is stiff. He has fallen in love with this woman who lives in Copenhagen, and anguish is visiting him.

Fabrice returns with a herb jar labelled basilic and a packet of papers. There is an abstract watercolour above the table. I see a goat dancing with a woman in a red dress, Max says.

Me: A matador. The cape is draped over his shoulder, his sombrero hung low, he's escorting a woman home.

Guy did that, Fabrice says. In daycare.

Max: I think he should change his name to Daycare and have a show.

Fabrice: I saw this drawing of a house by Magritte. I was with Connie. We were this far from it. There were two holes in the top. He had stuck it on his door, then decided to move it. The only colour was a food stain in the sky.

Me: Was it good?

No, but we knew we were in love.

Max: I dont like how impersonal we're being.

Fabrice: I think we're being very personal.

Fabrice pulls an LP from its sleeve. Records, Max says. I take a draw as Fabrice begins to sing in translation.

Who is this.

Léo Ferré: 'Avec le Temps'. The French, Fabrice says, love words. The English are for melody.

And what about the Japanese.

What about them.

There's something Japanese about that piece by Daycare. That woman reminds me.

Everything reminds you.

Of what.

Of love.

That's if youre an optimist.

Fabrice: The Japanese have a little Green Gables. Dont you love that. How they fall in love with this free spirit.

When Léo Ferré ends, Fabrice puts on Miles Davis. Technology, Fabrice says, is a backward nostalgia.

Say what?

I dont know.

This is Miles? Max asks.

Fabrice says, Miles was in his seventies. Miles saw the next wave.

He was the Magritte of jazz.

Fabrice, pointing up to illustrate: Wayne Gretzky. How he changed hockey. Within the rules he performed a new game.

Max, still looking at the Daycare painting: The Gretzky of Green Gables.

He has a, have you seen it? A rock in a bedroom.

Fabrice lifts his head to be sick. You must excuse me.

We take a shoulder each and help him to the toilet.

I am really sorry about this.

We lay his head on a folded towel on the corner of the sink. Max says, and maybe the bathroom reminds him of a sauna, but it comes with an air of the confessional: The problem with making art comes when your critical eye grows larger than your talent.

This I take to explain why Fabrice is a civil servant.

And he has Guy.

I've got a Guy, Max says.

But you dont have a woman. And he's lost Connie.

I've got a woman. She's just a ways away. I need a passport.

So what are you going to do.

Marry her. If her divorce comes through.

We finish our beer and check in on Fabrice. Sorry, Fabrice says, his head still on the sink. He waves us on, Make a home, please.

But we say good night.

We leave Max's car and walk along Freshwater Road, past the dark high schools that we both attended. Nothing on the roads now but fast taxis and police cruisers. Max stops on the corner of Barnes Road to pee in some bushes. He stares intently at a lit window.

Winston's up, he says.

This is Winston's?

That's the house made of burnt wood.

We are drawn to the light. As if we had been alone a long time and this, a welcome beacon. It seems natural to step into Winston's driveway and along the wet grass under a burning screen window. We lean against the clapboard and listen. We are listening to a man explain something to a woman. You can hear the fridge door close — it must have been open, and the spout of a milk carton, the clink of a teaspoon taking turns in two cups. What does Winston say to his new wife? It's the tone. The tone of a man used to a child crying at night. The stirring of honey. Every night this goes on, a continuation Max and I have forgotten. There is just a line of wet bushes separating us from the road and I see Max's head tilt back and touch the aluminum window frame. He is listening hard to this tender progress. There is no grief here.

Deep in My Brother

Junior: I saw a blur in the tall grass in back of the garage. I went after it. I found this litter in a torn cardboard box. I grabbed one and he bit me and I gaffed him by the scruff and took him to the van and fed him milk and hamburger. He was this tiny package of bone and fur and teeth and I went back to get a brother for him but the litter was gone and a couple of the grey pups were flattened like rats on the parking lot. I saw the bitch once carrying a dead one off into the woods and she was so dehydrated and resigned with her pink teats flapping, so I kept Trapper. His origins are wild but he has a pet for a mother. So, fifty animal and fifty pet and he's so fucking loyal, arent you Trapper?

I remember my father's car gently accelerating. It's dark, there are flashes of snow in the headlights. At the crest of a hill above

the Tourist Lodge, overlooking Corner Brook, dark and twinkling in linked units descending slopes to a smoking pulp mill
glowing with an inner grey light.

Dad: On three I want you to slam your hands on the dash.

The orange needle in its hot yellow dome wiggling on
forty miles an hour.

I slap my hand against the pebbled glove box. I havent
understood. Junior is braced. My father tramps on the brake.
There is no traffic. The car slides on greasy snow. I lurch towards
the windshield. Junior catches me on the shoulder and chin. He
saves me. It's so fast, but my father has seen this, though he
doesnt speak of it. He is testing the brakes in the snow.

I'm coming to realize there are no new thoughts. There are
thoughts that are in minority, thoughts that rule. These thoughts
gently replace each other, snow melting and falling again.

Junior had to explain to the police that they had been
drinking and Rory Wyatt went off in a canoe and they didnt
miss him until they were going back into Jody Miller's. It's been
two days now and theyve got a net across the river. Rory was
always a bit dense. He lost an eye when a pellet ricocheted.

But that could have been any of us.

Yeah, that was bad luck.

Once, I caught Rory rifling quarters out of Mom's bank
with a knife. I had the boys in and when we left Rory wasnt
with us. Found him in the kitchen up on the counter, jimmying
out quarters. Just told him to get out and never come back in.

Junior: Never knew that.

Never told anyone.

Would have beat the face off him.

Was taking his grandmother's pension cheques.

I heard about that.

What a case.

He's a asshole.

They were dragging the lake for him. Gill net so he doesnt float out to sea. Rory Wyatt, gone for good.

Me: What have you got done to the bunk?

So my feet can stick over.

You sawed out a chunk.

They were getting cut off, Gabe. I was waking up with dead feet. I know exactly what a amputee must feel.

I just come in to microwave an egg.

Sure, be my guest. You too, Mom?

Mom: No, I'm watching from a crack in the door.

She dont trust the microwave, Gabe. Got to keep it in here.

Dad has a bookcase for us each, hey.

Does he?

It's in three pieces.

Oh yeah. I knew that.

Me: What do you think of that.

Well, what else was he gonna do.

He could have just made one bookcase.

Easier to build in units. Then he thought of you, me and Bruce and made three. If it had been sounder to make one he would have. He built one bunk bed. Three and the wood dont warp. I've never done an egg before.

He built one bunk bed because two beds wouldnt fit in the room. You know what your problem is?

Only problem I got is people telling me what I can't do.

You won't listen, June, except when it's related to you. You won't think of someone else. Or acts of generosity. It's all what you can get and if someone hampers you youre pissed off.

When did you become a sociologist.

Just telling you what I'm seeing.

I used to come down and pound you.

I havent forgot. There was one time with an air rifle, Rory cocked it and fired it right into my ear.

And you let him off with it.

I'm not confrontational.

Is this, like, a eulogy to Rory?

Elegy. Youre saying that as if youre pissed off.

It would have been better if you'd kicked the shit out of him and what the fuck's different in a elegy and a eulogy.

Mom: Boys.

You know who made the air rifles, Gabe? Daisy. With a little bull's-eye in the D.

You used to come in here and say Gabe, I need you for backup. I'm fighting Joe Callahan up the Bean and his brothers are gonna be there.

Joe had four brothers, and Bruce was useless.

You know, I asked Dad what he thought of coming home and having to belt us?

He gave me the belt.

You remember your own ass.

I didnt deserve it.

Me: He said he hated it. Didnt know what he'd find. Mom tells him a story and he has to go get the belt. All he's doing is coming home. What did he do to deserve it.

Never thought of what he deserved.

Mom: I wasnt a very good mother.

Look, there's a hole in the wall from where Mom swung a chair.

Mom: I'm not proud of that.

Just plastered over.

Junior: I can hear the closet door now. You'd be bawling. Like when we took you in on the train in summer. Me, Dad, Bruce and you, picking berries and shooting grouse and bagging a caribou. Thought you were too good for all that. Your little hands giving out from carrying. Had to tie your wrists to the meat. I can tell you exactly where there's a moose now, Gabe. On the Yellow Marsh. I could lead you right to him.

You probably got him tied on.

Mom: Is it okay that it's beeping?

It's ninety seconds for an egg. You have to break the yolk. You have to cover it with paper or it'll blow up.

Look, Mom's shaking her head.

Mom: I dont know how you can eat it.

I got a cabin now in the Yellow Marsh and the train is gone, so I walk in. A lot of people are on all-terrain vehicles, Gabe. Well, I'll walk, thank you very much. That's what Old Phonse did before the Bullet and that's what I'll do. Train used to kill five hundred moose a year, Gabe. I got no time for trikes — what I wouldnt mind getting is a pony. Though I'd have to grow hay then. But yes, next year it might be a pony, a brown one.

There's a book with a piece of sandpaper sticking out of it on Junior's desk, the physics of footings and cement foundations.

Me: Dad made that closet door. He made the bunk beds and the desk and the bedroom door and the base of that lamp and the pelmets and half the house.

Junior: You wanna go in the warehouse?

The what?

Mom: Junior calls the woods the warehouse.

Cause you can get anything you want in there.

You can get cement?

You got to buy cement.

Let me eat my egg. You want an egg?

I dont like to eat in the morning.

I look through the transit set up at the dining-room window.

Mom: You have to push against the plant. Like that German actor who always hid behind fronds.

I lean into the eyepiece and eat my egg. I see the black slant of Pynn's roof. Down the Valley to the right of the mill. Up onto Humber Heights. The Kingdom Hall getting shingled. That bright yellow is a line of portable toilets.

Junior was amazed at the roof trusses, she says. He knows all he needs to build the roof on his cabin. I had Reg in, Reg delivers the groceries.

I know Reg, Mom. He's been delivering for twenty-five years.

He knows I'm Jehovah's Witness. He said he wouldnt have thought you'd see anything through all the telephone wires. I mean it's a mile away. He wanted to know if all the Witnesses got a transit. Old Phonse came in for a look and said, So that's Premier Drive. He'd never been on Premier Drive.

She is standing behind me with wet hands held up so they won't drip. There are bubbles of dish detergent on her fingers. She's washing the aluminum pie plates.

Youre washing the plates.

Junior, she says, used to squash them in his hand like this. I caught him and said, You know I reuse them, June. I could tell he was crestfallen, so I gave him a window. I said, I reuse them until they wear out. He started asking me then if it was time and I'd hold one up to the light and say, Yes boy, go for it.

She doesnt use the dryer function on the dishwasher because she finds they dry off enough on their own, although sometimes the cutlery is dribbly. There's a photograph in the album of when the washer arrived, still in its cardboard box, in the porch.

I didnt want the power bill to be too different and youre starting to wish he hadnt bought it. Your Dad says there's been no difference because there should be a bit with the engine going instead of me going, although now I dont fill the sink with hot water three times a day. I figure, I save an hour a day on washing, so that's an extra day's work a week, and I have noticed I'm getting more done.

She uses Dad's calculator to work out the price of toilet paper and it's perfect. The toilet paper companies are colluding to make it difficult to work out. You can't go now by just how many rolls there are because some have less sheets per roll. But Dad showed her the division.

I ask, What about two-ply versus one-ply?

Oh, I only get two-ply now. It's not the same as when you were all here, I mean you boys used to eat it. But your Dad said the one-ply was too thin. And now of course they make the two-ply as thin as the one-ply was, but I've got no control over that.

Last night in the yard she showed me seeds tumbling out of columbine into her hand. Are they the same as in the packet? Oh, yes, she said, except they'll all be the same colour as this flower, not mixed. She said, isnt the garden plodgy, like a sandy beach. We've had awful rain.

I remember standing on the soft bottom. On decaying bog. Arms outstretched as if balancing. There is no alarm in my drowning body. It was Junior's idea to leave my lifejacket. I can see the surface about four feet up. The square silhouette of the raft. It's a calm day, the light jiggling. It's hot up there. I make no attempt for it. It never occurs to me to struggle. I stand, bubbles pressing under my nose. But there is no need to breathe. I look at the light at the top of the darkness.

There is something strong around my waist and I bend. There is a movement of water. I dont like this, I'm pushed upwards. I am being towed some place. The force of raw light breaks over me. I've broken into a lightness and it's burning my throat.

Fuck, Gabe. You won't tell? I got to shore and looked around and saw your bubbles.

It's cut up?

It's all sawed.

Did you pay in sawlogs?

Junior: Nobody gets my wood but me.

We drive up to Old Phonse's. We've called him Old Phonse since we were kids. We heard Alphonse as Old Phonse. Trapper with his paws on the dash, steadying.

Junior: Old Phonse told me I could keep the wood there till the fall. But Dad said I should get it out now. There it is.

Now that's a load of wood.

Beauties on thirty-degree hills, Gabe. No one else could get em. Old Phonse said I was crazy. Junior English, he said. Youre leaving some tops in the woods. I said to Old Phonse, You got a problem with my tops? Old Phonse: No, June, just it's a waste. Well, like I'm gonna haul out a three-inch top. See, Gabe? Lift a piece and find me rot or shake. You could cut cue sticks out of it.

The wood runs true.

He tells me I'm entitled to six thousand board feet. You go down to city hall and get a permit for twenty-one dollars.

We load up the truck, Junior collecting the stick dividers and bundling them carefully.

I say, Do you remember the raft.

You sure are into remembering.

Just if you remember what I remember.

What I remember is getting in shit, Gabe. It's not in my best interest to remember.

But you remember things all the time.

That's not the same. I'm remembering because I'm reminded. You just remember for the sake of remembering. It doesnt illustrate. Okay, something I remember — Mr Wyatt hanging Rory by a belt loop from a hook in the kitchen ceiling. You ever see that?

Yeah.

You were there once, hey. Rory hanging paralysed. Well that's what I want to do with my cabin. Want to build it with a garage door and a stone floor so I can drive my Pocahontas right to the centre, under the I beam. I'll have a hook I can put a winch and haul the engine right out of her.

We buy a posthole digger in Canadian Tire for eighteen dollars. It's like two big spoons.

You jam it down, scoop it out. I used them all the time in Florida. I'm gonna fence in all four acres. Black spruce. With the bark on. That's what they got over the bay. Dad says he dont see it. Thinks it'll rot. I say what does he know, is he a farmer? He says it has more to do with the ground. You like my new boots?

Junior drove a branch through his first pair.

Woman said there's a one-year warranty. Said if you melt them on the stove it's no good. What if I drive a chainsaw through them? No, she says. I said, What are you gonna do with the old ones? Send them back to the manufacturer. Mind if I take the laces out of them? Free laces, bonus. That kind of upset her.

Junior wedges the digger between his lumber and the wheel well.

We'll unload this, have a bite and I'll take you to Bottle Cove. Tomorrow you help me with a culvert, okay?

Sure thing.

Trapper anchors himself on the seat. Front paws on the dash, nose wedged along it with his snout stuck to the window. There's a line of dried snout marks on the glass. He falls asleep up there like that, Gabe. Coming up from Florida he'd get like that and I'd jerk the brake and turn — he'd fall off to the floor and scrabble up and get in position again, but this time give me a dirty look. Hoo hoo.

He flicks Trapper's ears inside out, turns to me and says, Convertible.

It's gonna be sun all day and sun tomorrow, Gabe. The best way to know what weather's coming is to dart outside just as it's getting dark and look west or whichever way the wind is, take a good look at the cloud formation and then at 8:20 on the Weather Network you get the satellite picture. Ignore what buddy is telling you, just stare at the pattern of cloud, study the ridge of low pressure and the fronts and what's coming up from Maine and what's over Labrador and you can figure out weather for the next three days.

Junior hauls up an envelope from under Trapper's paw and
wags it. I got fifteen hundred dollars from the US this week,
American. That's two grand Canadian and more if I wait cause
our dollar's gonna go down, Gabe. Hard to wait, though, but I
like it sitting there, making money. That's my settlement. I had
a lawsuit, two years old. Remember me telling you about a car
I T-boned at a intersection in Daytona?

I was down there.

Oh yeah. You came just after. Well, that's where I got the
nose. I was speeding but I had the green. Broke a girl's legs. She
was driving a Jetta, got a strong frame. I told you this? Lucky I
only broke her legs. I was in a plastic Geo, like they weigh
eight hundred pounds. A second earlier, and she wouldve T-
boned me, and I wouldnt be here. Anyway, you know all that. I
dont want to fucking bore you.

A thick white scar across the bridge of his nose. I have the
same nose except for the scar. Junior didnt have medical insurance, so he cleaned the wound and placed a square of gauze on
it and covered it with a strip of duct tape and left it. When I
arrived he'd had the duct tape on fourteen days. He had a
severe headache and his nose was puffed up. When he took off
the tape he had a pale square of skin across the bridge. He
washed his face and I swabbed the deep black scab with Dettol
and it was still on when I left a week later. Two years, he says. I
let the lawyer go for it. Whatever I got, he got half.

At a red he muscles Trapper over and takes out his gear
from the glove box. He's given up cigarettes, but tokes about
nine times a day. With a lighter he heats up a sewing needle

between his knees. He smears oil on a paper with the hot needle, then sprinkles tobacco over it. The red turns to green and
he drives, steering with his knees pressed to the wheel. I've
been toking right along with him.

Dad found a bag of garbage just down here, he says, at the
corner. It was suspicious, like what was garbage doing out here.
So he opened it up and it was full of new clothes, dry cleaning
hangers. He put it in the paper. Had a whack of calls — it was
end of the month and people moving — a bag had fallen out.
So he had them describe the contents, and they were all
wrong. Dad couldnt believe people did that, put clothes in a
garbage bag. Like, he would never do that. You put clothes in
a suitcase. You put garbage in a garbage bag.

Anyway the owner phoned. But still everybody called up,
people who were just realizing they were missing things, and
they wouldnt believe it wasnt theirs, that someone else had
claimed it. They thought they were the only ones who put
clothes in garbage bags. They werent even sure what they'd
lost, just that something seemed missing.

Junior had called me from a Daytona payphone and said come
on down. There's a teak sailboat we can salvage in the Bahamas.
Sail it up to St John's and sell it. I said, Is that you, June?

Funny, hey? he'd said. You can know a voice half a world
away. And halfway is as far as you can get from anything.

The roads swirl round like eggs in a bowl. And now the house.
A white smoke at the chimney and the kitchen window with

no curtain. Mom busy at the sink. Her long white hair. What did she say? I won't be one of those women who cut their hair short. Junior guns it past the house.

Any other truck, Gabe, and this load would snap a spring. But this truck I bought off a Pocahontas Indian in Florida. He blew the motor and I traded him a Honda Civic. Only problem is it dont like winter. Not built for Newfoundland, built for Texas. Let's drop in on Old Phonse.

Old Phonse parked in at Employment and Immigration. His chip trailer sign says FRIES N DRINK $2. The N is backwards. Old Phonse says, Boys, youre early — I'm only just getting the fat boiled up. Maybe I should come with you, yes, now that's what I'll do.

He presses his eye against the fly screen to check Employment and Immigration.

Nobody gonna come out now till dinnertime. Fucking big fat lady comes out and I knows what she's gonna say and I says to her before she has a chance: I know, missus, you dont like em hard — well I knows how she does like em, the cunt on that all she wants is her cunt filled and her welfare cheque theyre in there all day getting money and coming out with the hungry cunt hanging off em.

Phonse, boy.

Yes, I'll shut up now. I'll come down with you if you got room. How you doing, Gabe, you still seeing that Nazi? Yes, now I knows she's not a Nazi but she comes from that extraction.

I'm not seeing her. I'm not seeing anyone.

That's good, you can never trust em, once a Nazi, you know, it's in your blood — they might on the outside be right apologetic but it's seething in em, hey, twist the bayonet right in your guts, or that's the Nips, pry open your ribs. I got a good knife now, June, got a ridge in it so to let the blood out. Good for the moose. Only joking boy, come and have a look at my spuds I picked em this morning — see my hands are stained with the peeling em, hey? I got to use bleach to get em white again I'm like a old nigger with my hands, but come now you try that.

Old Phonse hands me a raw chip of potato. I crunch it.

Theyre some good, arent they. I does em right good now.

It's good potato.

Junior: You got to blanch em first.

Old Phonse: That makes em taste not fresh.

Junior: That's how I like em.

That potato havent been out the ground a hour. Malt vinegar, they says it's addictive. I'm gonna get it to put on the chips. Next year I'll be serving hamburgers. I want to get ground beef through my cousin in the Codroy, or what I'd like to use is moose, but then youre dealing with Health Department.

There is a sign: If you like the chips, tell your friend; if you dont, tell me.

Old Phonse: June, you got all that wood in one trip, that's some truck.

He twists the knob on the rusty propane tank. Then he

picks up an old Lee Enfield from the floor of the chip trailer and climbs aboard.

In case I get a irate customer.

We drive down to Bartlett's Point, past the Brothers' residence. Trapper is clinging on to the wood in back. Old Phonse wants to give the Brothers a needle and bury them.

Christian Brothers and Nazis.

He shakes his head.

Junior hauls off at a groc & conf, Trapper lurches forward and smacks into the rear window. Old Phonse ducks in and comes out with a case of beer. Then we take a left and dip off the pavement onto Junior's Road. Trapper leaps off and runs ahead. Junior has to back up on the last hundred feet over a brook.

Got to get a sign that says Junior's Road.

Old Phonse: No, you dont want a sign, June.

I'm sizing up a sign on Juniper Road, Phonse. Wouldnt take much to change Juniper.

Juniper, Old Phonse says. You dont want it to say Juniper. You say Junior's Road five hundred times, and everyone will say it. If you got a sign people will resent it.

I got a pond named after me at the cabin. June's Pond.

You got a sign for that.

Dont need a sign.

Well, that's what I'm saying.

Old Phonse rolls down the window.

That culvert aint gonna hold in spring, June.

I need a twenty-four-inch diameter pipe and I know just where to get one out by Deer Lake. That and a load of gravel. Gabe's gonna help me.

Lots of gravel in town now, I say. They're building these walking trails. You could drive up at midnight and fill your truck with gravel.

Junior shakes his head. Gabe, you dont know the value of things. I can go down to Lundrigan's with a ten-dollar bill, sit right here and watch through the rear-view at a guy loading Pocahontas with gravel and I'd get a loonie passed back to me through the window.

Old Phonse opens a beer and passes it over. He has the rifle between his legs, muzzle to the floor. It's not even nine in the morning. He holds up a hand for a general cease in discussion.

He says, There's only a devil, okay boys? and the devil is good. God is the devil.

At least, he says, that's how I sees it.

He drops the hand and we crank open the doors, step down, stretch our backs, and study Junior's foundation. He's dug, with pick and shovel, to a depth of six feet. There are batter boards to keep the sides of the foundation true. The boards are notched on the corners.

Old Phonse: You talk about the value of things. How long it take you to trench that? You been at that all summer. You couldve had a backhoe in here at thirty dollars a hour and had that done in a afternoon. See, June, I've done all this.

He spreads his hand over the ground.

Junior: That would have been a good idea.

He's admitting to this. He points to a narrow clearing. See the surveying line? I had Dad up here with the transit. Phonse, I wished I had a shotgun. If I had a gun I would've shot myself.

Old Phonse: Your father's got an opinion.

We park the beer on Junior's picnic table. Old Phonse slowly creeps up on the plot of potatoes. He steals up as if the potatoes might run away.

I never seen this before, he says. Look, Gabe, at that.

He crouches and holds up five pale stalks between his fingers. He hides his face, then wipes off a laugh.

You got like six spuds a square inch, June? No wonder they havent flowered.

Leave me alone.

Youre some farmer.

They'll be all right.

You gonna put on clapboard?

Board on board.

That's a good way to go if you got a lot of board.

I got six thousand feet.

Got your limit.

I was gonna cut a deal with Gabe. Get his wood and we'd split it. Whatever you want, Gabe. I'll pay your permit. If you want birch or big spruce or pine. Three thousand each.

Dont be doing that, Gabe.

Shut up now, Phonse.

Old Phonse slaps his hands on his thighs. Junior, you got the spot. You can look out over the Bay of Islands. Why go to Weebald when you can see it out your picture window? Look, you can shoot your moose out the back door (he shoots an imaginary moose). Set your slips and cut the finest kind of wood. Grow a ton of spuds and cabbage and turnip. You got the set-up, boy.

Junior digs out a melted lighter from some stones. He says, Last week I found this burnt into my picnic table. I know the fucker. It's that old fucker down there. I want to blow in his front door. I told Dad and he said dont do that. Just make sure he's not in the house and go down. Put the lighter in his mailbox. Then he'll know that I know. But this is what I want to do: I want to shit three times into a baggie and freeze it with the lighter stuck in it. Put that in his mailbox.

No, boy, Junior you can't be doing that. He's your neighbour, right? When I shot Vatcher I couldnt stand looking at the doghouse. I had to shoot him. Arsehole was out of him for the last six months. Your father shot him actually. Dog catcher he uses gas but it burns up their lungs and vet he charges sixty dollars for a needle. So I had Al shoot him up at the dump. Every night after from the kitchen I'd see Vatch's doghouse, empty. I got too sad, so I doused it in gasoline and burned it after supper. Well, it burned down the neighbour's fence too and half his lawn. I was too sad to do anything. He called the fire department and he was right to do it. I mean, I shouldve told him I was gonna burn down the doghouse.

Junior: Some people never become themselves because theyre afraid to be fools.

Old Phonse: That's the big difference between cities and the wild, June. You have to make your own happenings in the wild. You have to act if you want one moment to stand out from another. The sun, he says. It aint even going to go behind a cloud today. And your father, he says, has a unrelenting concentration.

We unload the wood and dart down to Bottle Cove. Junior drives Pocahontas onto the beach. He says, This is where I slept the first three months I was in Daytona, Phonse. Right on the beach at high tide. It's called the littoral zone. That's where most of life on earth lives, hey Gabe. Right here. That's where I lived. Gabe came down when I was living there. Only one to come down. There's a slant to a beach you can feel when youre asleep. Slipping off into water. That's where they had the first races in Daytona. It used to be a beach race before it went commercial. I had to paint my van white, it was so hot. I bought a gallon of exterior and a brush.

Old Phonse: You was like a animal changing colour.

I was feral, Junior says. I had escaped captivity.

I strip off to my underwear as they talk about Daytona. I walk into the water. Old Phonse: Now what's he up to?

My feet hurt on small round stones. Junior says, Go for it, man. Trapper stops at the waterline. Old Phonse: Never swum in salt water.

I'm surprised at the number of fishing boats. Mostly dories, orange with green bottoms, with 40 Yamaha outboards.

I can hear Old Phonse talking to Junior. Yammy, he says, is motor of choice. Same as a Mariner but cheaper. Gearing up for some jigging.

You can feather for herring, hey, and catch cod. Sly way to get your fish.

The water warm and shallow. There is a man leaning over one boat with goggles on. He is looking at something on the bottom, or maybe he's checking out his own boat. The stones turn to seaweed. Crescent of a fish caught in a gill net. I lean into a wave and swim.

They find Rory's body washed up on the shore down by Jody Miller's house. It's on AM radio when we're driving home.

I remember, Old Phonse says, when you beached that kayak down at Jody's. You were starving. For three years, hey Gabe, June had beaten the two-man canoes.

Junior: I was so hungover.

Me: Mom had to get him out of bed. He drank a glass of juice and Dad tied the kayak on the roof rack.

We listened to the race on radio. Junior English way ahead now coming through Pasadena straits. Junior English on the whirlpool narrow and. Now we've lost sight of English. He should be through those birch and ripping along Shelbert Island. No boats on the river at all now. Nothing. Drs Hillier and Lundrigan way up river, by the boom. Theyre gaining and rounding the steadies. First of the canoes shooting the rapids. Junior English nowhere in sight. Two more canoes now. Oh. And here is Junior English! In fourth place and quickly gaining. Passing two canoes.

But he had to settle for second. The doctors made the bridge a length ahead of him.

Junior: I thought I had enough of a lead to dart in to Jody Miller's and make a sandwich. But I misjudged it.

Mom is making relish. Parboiling garden tomatoes, six pounds at a time. Then peeling them. She punctures the tomato near the stem and hauls a strip off. The rest of the skin follows. For green chutney you can leave the skins on.

At supper there's a phone call and my father answers. He listens then says, Who wants to know.

It's a wrong number.

As he sits back down my mother says, You always do that, answer with a question.

And why not?

Youre doing it again.

He says, When Pilate asked Jesus if he was King of the Jews, what did he answer?

Youre not going to goad me.

My father's first belief is suspicion.

Who is it you say I am, he says.

There's a thread on the head of a burnt match. He finds it, holds the thread and pulls. The head of the match snaps off.

But he was twisting the base of the match between his fingers.

My father opens a bottle of port and pours four glasses. That moose, he says, will dissolve in your mouth. He stands and we stand. This, he says, a gift from Old Phonse and his wife. For our thirty-fifth year.

Me: Oh, last week. The seventh.

The ninth. The ninth day of the ninth month and our sons can't remember.

Junior: Are you allowed to toast anniversaries?

Mom: Yes.

Junior: I didnt think you celebrated anything except Easter.

The Bible says to celebrate the marriage.

We drink and sit. My father swirls the port.

Terrific legs.

I look at my father. He is exactly twice my age.

Is that right? he says.

That means you were like me when you had me.

Youre only twenty-six, I thought.

I'm thirty-one.

Well, I'll toast to that.

Mom: I'll congratulate you all for getting older.

My mother will not speak of the scar on her left shoulder blade. I have seen it as we peeled logs for the cabin. Down to her bra in the heat, bent over the logs on the sawhorses. The scapula flexing the scar. The scar is six inches long, thick as a finger. As if her shoulder blade or her bones were placed inside her skin that way, and zippered up.

All she said was, your father waited for me. I was gone a year and he waited.

I thought the San was a beach. I thought she had taken a year to tan and heal on a warm, sandy beach.

I am looking at a photograph of their wedding. Outside

the gothic doors of a Catholic church.

It's not Catholic. We were married Anglican.

But it has a saint's name.

It's not just Catholics that sanctify.

I thought the idea of saints was a Catholic one.

There were saints before the Catholics started canonizing.

Do the Witnesses name their churches?

It says nothing in the Bible about naming your place of worship. Names are the work of man.

But if youre going to church, and youre telling a friend, what would you call it.

Theyre all called Kingdom Hall. This new one, they started the foundation when the ground had thawed.

Do they always build new Halls?

In third world countries they'll renovate a building. Often a church that's closed.

Dad: And what if it's in the shape of a cross.

They'll remove any decorations, a cross outside.

But most churches are built on the cross.

Its shape wouldnt be significant, Al. We wouldnt praise the architecture.

Well I say that's an interesting contradiction.

It's not what you say that matters. To me: I've got something to show you.

She leads me into their bedroom. In a wooden jewellery box beneath a tray. She takes out a clear plastic bag. There are three locks of braided ginger hair.

I havent told anyone about this but youre always wanting

to know what's up so I'm telling you this is here for when I go. There's one each. I had four, but I buried one in the back-yard for Bruce. Your Dad will probably want this one because it's got the most red in it. And these are both the same so you can choose.

She is staring at the ginger fondly.

When did you cut them.

Oh, they must be ten years old. At least. I dont know what made me think of them. When I cut them, knowing that was it, I was going grey.

She has, in the past, looked in the mirror and been shocked.

We sit in the living room after supper, the new bookcase flank-ing the far wall. Dad watching the taped Business Report. Mom with her feet up, licking her finger as she pushes through Daniel.

Junior, quietly: We'll get that culvert in the morning.

Come on.

Yellow grass. The rock showing through. Up the trail by the Fire Break.

You know who I am?

Youre Rory.

You know?

Youre Rory Wyatt.

Yeah. Rory Wyatt. That's me.

He tells me to kneel in the grass. I know he's Rory Callahan from the Bean. He's pissing over the small willows.

The ground has a wink of crushed beer bottles.

Gabe, your brother's an asshole.

He turns and I get a splash of hot urine.

Go on, you crybaby. And who am I?

Rory Wyatt.

Rory Wyatt in the car when I go off the road.

New Year's. You never got in shit for it.

I had to fix the car, June. Spent all winter fibreglassing.

They were way easier on you.

You said to me, Dont drive past your lights.

I said, Whatever you do, dont dent Dad's car. And you come
home with it totalled.

Dont drive past your lights. A speed faster than light. Faster
than the eye can react. Perhaps fate and destiny are contingent
on light. There is a beam of the standard, the known, right up
to the brink of change. A filament tows you unerringly to a
destination. Trunk stacked with beer. I am passing a slow driver
and slice into a bank of snow in the meridian. Why the hell am
I passing him? Back of the car swings. We watch the car grind
sideways. I've locked the brakes. We slide into the white. The
white is a dry powder filling a ditch. We plunge into the ditch.
This long moment a soft transition into abruptness. The front
digs in solid, a hard jolt. Headlights spin the hill, heads of
bushes capped in snow. We roll upside down, hesitate on a corner of the roof, settle back. Dangling in our seat belts. I can feel
my own weight straining the belt. I let go of the clasp and hit

the roof. Shit I'm wet, Rory says. We are drenched in beer.

We crawl out the web of broken back window. Sparks are sizzling around the motor. We throw snow on it. We douse the sparks in snow. Cars have stopped, headlights tracking through falling snow.

I gotta stay here.

We'll report it, Gabe.

And tell my father, okay?

I wait. Cars stop. Snow continues in their headlights. No one tells my father. The beer freezes on my sweater and I can't feel my hands or feet.

We tilt the raft. Mom and Dad at the cabin talking to Old Phonse and his wife. We stand on the edge, the raft tears off the water. It keeps tilting and smacking. High. Too high to run back on. It flips. The raft closes down on me like a lid.

I'm giving you a lift home, son.

A stranger drives me to the front door. There are modest fireworks over Crow Hill. I hear the report of shotguns. In the porch, laughter. Junior leans into me, his mouth open as if in whispered warning, his chin pulled in until all I see are the black spelks of his beard. A menacing blackness. He lets out a large burp that smells of digestion. Then he farts.

Youre fucking gross.

He's laughing. He can't believe his own luck. Did you dent the car, Gabe?

I totalled it.

I watch my brother's eyes. His back arches, and he laughs up at the ceiling. Are you ever. Gonna be in shit.

Dad in the kitchen, having heard from Mom on their way to a party. He leans on the Formica counter, his arms crossed.

Well, he says, happy new year.

Fire-Eater

Are you interested in going?

No.

Can you maybe think about it before saying no?

Okay.

And when I've thought about it — I often say no where Lydia will say yes — I say, I'll go down with you and stay an hour.

You dont have to.

No, I'd like to.

I lift her wiper blades and stroke the new snow off her rear window. She says, I need a scraper.

Have you noticed, I say, how often men get into the passenger seat?

I reach underneath her hands on the steering wheel, while she is reversing, and press the rear defogger. I would love to meet the person who invented the rear defogger. That's a sensitive touch.

Lydia parks on the sidewalk in front of the old hall. She was allowed to park here for meetings when she was on the board, and now she still parks here. She gives me a look to say she knows.

We run down the stairs fast to the Ship.

She says, That's Leo.

Leo up front, leaning his chair slightly on its black metal legs. He is drawing the woman next to him with felt markers. In this light Leo's eyes are nothing. Lydia buys me a beer. She says she met Leo at the dress rehearsal party, he just stuck out his hand and introduced himself, and Lydia realized, oh this guy is new.

Hello Leo, I say.

Why hi.

Leo has a Tennessee flavour. He wears horn-rimmed glasses. His hand is small and warm. The woman next to him introduces herself, Sandra. The music is loud so I talk to Sandra because she's closest. She's into development studies, has spent three years in Botswana.

I know something about Botswana. It's about where my liver is? I point to my liver. More like your groin, she says. Landlocked. Yes. Gaborone. I say, Have you read Norman Rush? Yes. Norman is the husband of the supervisor of her project. She's read *Mating* twice and thinks of it anthropologically. She says, It's very accurate of my situation — you should read *Whites*, it's even better.

Sandra has been clenching her thin fist on the table. Taut skin on a strongly defined face, long brown hair, my age. The eyes are slightly crazy. Or, she has come through a craziness.

She says, Tell me, Gabriel. If a woman was bouncing on top of you in bed and you suddenly realized her breasts were implants, would you tell her? Like, would you be disgusted?

Would I tell her?

Would it turn you off.

I dont think it would matter.

That's great. That is so great. She turns to Leo. I'm definitely getting them.

I interrupt. Youre getting implants?

Yeah.

Lydia looks at me.

Look, I'm not suggesting you get implants. I think your breasts are perfect.

But I'm wearing a push-up bra.

Your size is beautiful.

Oh, youre sweet, Gabe. But it's for myself.

I hear Leo telling Lydia, Broken up with my girlfriend. She wanted to get married but I'm devoted to art. Lydia leaning over the table to hear him. And I realize I am leaning into Sandra. We are both leaning to strangers.

I angle back and touch Lydia's leg. She pushes her thigh towards me. Leo turns to me.

And youre an artist too?

I'm writing a novel.

Well, that's an artist. It must be exciting, when so many

novels are being made into movies.

Yes, Lydia says. But Gabe thinks movies undermine books. Words are themselves and not other things, is what Gabe says.

But wouldnt it be fun, Leo says, to see something you write transformed?

Sandra: It's better to see the movie first. And then read the book.

Lydia: I'm all for the transformation.

The frame of Leo's glasses is two different colours. One side burgundy, the other charcoal. This makes his eyes appear to be different colours. The colouring of most eyes is not memorable. The only eyes I know right now are Sandra's and Lydia's. Mine are green. Eye colour is overrated as a descriptive device. It is good for passports. A technical observation, a fingerprint. They have an ID scanner now for irises.

Leo's hair is brown and tufted. He doesnt comb it. He has a tuft left in the front that will soon be an island. But right now he is defined. The hair and neat beard define him.

His eyes. When I say eye colour is not a feature, I am not discounting the eyes themselves. I am not discounting personal expression.

I get up for a beer. John is at the bar. I'm light with him. I decide to be light and chatty. I have to make these kinds of decisions. I ask how he is.

In crisis.

His grey shirt and tie, sweater. Charcoals. Smiling uncomfortably. But this happens in life.

Me: What were you doing when you were thirty-one?

Yes, he says. That was a year of crisis too. I was in Victoria. Victoria is beautiful for one year. Then youre sick of it. I'd been overseas. Then I went to the prairies for a couple of years.

As John speaks, anxious looks over my shoulder.

He says, You and Lydia look great. She's so bold and courageous, isnt she?

And I see Agatha, his Agatha, with the film crowd in the corner.

Bold and courageous, he says. It doesnt fit her. Sounds like a clothing store for overweight women.

Weeks ago, Agatha told Lydia this: What John did I can't imagine anyone else doing to another person. Lydia (to me, as we're lying in bed): It must mean he wants to break up. But she wouldnt say what it was.

One of Lydia's hands in the dark.

Something sexual, I say.

Something perverse.

My mind opens up. Yes, I've been thinking, something to do with sperm. Smearing a possession with it. Giving her a vial.

Lydia's hand pauses to indicate disgust. But then she is released from a censor.

She says, Maybe he gave Agatha a videotape of himself having sex with someone else, with a man, a dog.

Yes, it's something like that. To make her not want to have sex with him.

He had sex with a dog.

He had sex with something like that.

It was a whole new side John revealed that was a little mean and incomprehensible to her.

Territory Agatha didnt know existed.

Was it malicious?

It was vengeful, with a hint of hope that backfired on him.

But right now at the bar as he sips a small drink I can't see it. John looks like he's done nothing wrong. He stares at Agatha, a woman he so clearly loves. He can look over at this woman and calculate her as you would the price of your groceries.

Agatha to the film crowd, Well who's making the movie?

The bar a pond of voices, those of certain pitch travelling over closer voices.

Tri Star, someone says.

Well Tri Star could give two shits about Newfoundland.

Did you read the book?

This is what Sandra is telling Lydia as I return with a beer and a brandy. The brandy is a surprise that will go down well. I can tell because of the fire in the grate and Lydia's back looks cold. I have a good look at Sandra's breasts. You need a fire in the periphery to enjoy a brandy. Naguib Mahfouz, Sandra is saying. I've been to Cairo, she says, but he's got it. I've read Edward Said for course work last year. I studied at the University of East Anglia? In Norwich? Ishiguro teaches there, and

Malcolm Bradbury, Ben Okri — he's not really Nigerian. I mean I've been to these places, not just travelled.

The band on break and Agatha and Helene join us. Helene is physical right to the surface of her fingers and cheekbones. I ask Leo, Is the party directly after? But he's turned to the women. Helene smiles and nods. A thick curl of white smoke snakes off her lip and Lydia sees the smile she gives me. Helene and I know each other from a sink at a party. Lydia, whispering: Helene walks a poodle on a chain, she wears a fur coat and a cigarette high on a gloved hand.

But I think all this funny and attractive and it's true that I kissed Helene at the sink (I was getting a glass of water) and then walked her around the lake, loaded, as fly fishermen tried to catch a tagged trout at dawn.

Leo, authoritatively: God is French. Because Dieu is a powerful word. God is too close to dog. And Dieu has that swearing aspect. God is not strong. Jesus, that's a good word. Do the French use Jesus?

Helene: They say Christ like crease.

That's strong too. All more powerful than God.

Agatha: I used to think that king, Croesus? I thought the phrase was rich as creases. Like you were rich enough to have an iron?

Sandra: I would never let him kiss me. Not even on the mouth.

Who? What have I missed getting this brandy?

I Am, Helene says. They used to call God, I Am.

Sandra and her clenched knuckles. She had said Said's name

only to let us know that she is engaged in the forum of ideas surrounding her work. She did not offer Said's name as content. She may be nuts, but she is not defensive. She retreats and marches. Her eye accepts everything about me.

Lot of eyes here tonight.

To Lydia, I am looking and speaking into Lydia's ear, Did you know that I could sleep with Sandra or Helene, I could sleep with Agatha. I do not say, I am still in a phase of physical yearning.

Lydia: You could sleep with all of them?

Would, let's say. A small impulse, but not even a twinge of desire, babe.

Lydia: I wouldnt sleep with Leo.

You wouldnt?

But I could sleep with Agatha. Or Sandra. Women, if you havent noticed, Gabe, are way different. We flirt. Flirtation is a different set of muscles and it's becoming apparent only women have them.

This, about eyes and personal expression, and I turn to Sandra and she knows that she's got my eye. Her eye has hooked me solid. Eyes are active muscles, they are not descriptive.

I catch myself thinking about John and Agatha. They stand as bride and groom at the top of cement stairs outside a white church, a rusty rail, but this is a veil on my brain. No one has told me the reason they have broken up. People should feel obliged to write out a statement of what happened, what went wrong, who was at fault and how they feel. A purely subjective, biased account. The statements kept together on file down at the archives, or at a website. So you can review the emotional history of anyone.

I am telling this to Sandra as we walk up the hill. As always the night has grown calmer and a little warmer, as if heat is coming off the earth. I tend to walk towards my house, even though another route that begins slightly at an angle may turn out shorter, my hunch compass tells me to go the way that initially points true.

I'm wondering about this.

I am walking Sandra home. We pass my house and keep walking. I dont want her at my house. We're having a conversation about everyone knowing everything. This is my belief: instinct about body language is a sophisticated, primitive knowledge, as old as sharks. Our intellect thinks it can hide true feeling through omissions in language, but it forgets the body is talking. What we hide is hidden only from our own brains. As long as someone is not practising obliviousness, they will know how you feel and what you feel for them.

This, of course, to let Sandra know that twenty percent of me wants to put my arm around her waist. Maybe it's all in the arm. If I could twist off the arm. I am thinking of hands cut off for thievery.

I had said to Lydia the other day, when she had said, sardonically, that I only like people who like me, that that was a very true thought and that we all succumb to it. Who hangs out with or likes people who despise them?

This because I am walking Sandra home and she invites me in and I climb her stairs, resigned to having a good time.

The curiosity, I say, of following what may happen. Is a joy.

Your nose is a joy button, she says.

There is a beer standing on her chrome shelf. Sandra closes the fridge so I won't see that nothing else is in it. She splits the beer. Art that makes you uncomfortable, she says. She is making a survey. I say, a recent movie, I hated it, but I'm glad to have seen it. The movie a relentless exploration of eros made painful. This done by combining elements of what is usually erotic with moments of perverse violence.

It's true that I could kiss her now. I could bend her away from the fridge, touch her bare neck, brush her small pushed-up breasts, and kiss that mouth, those crazy eyes. Again, about twenty percent, but it's not in the arm now.

Lydia, I said, I'm gonna go now. Hang on a little, babe. She presses my leg. No, it's been two hours and I've got to be up. She releases my leg. Okay, well, I'm gonna hang on and buy Leo a beer. Sandra: I'm gonna go too and Gabe can walk me up the hill.

I held the door as she looked down to button her coat, looked down and trusted the door was open and Lydia to the bar to buy the beer. John still staring across the bar, gently swirling his snifter an inch from his chin. Now she is talking to John.

Lydia: Have you kissed anyone?

Yes.

You kissed Sandra.

No. I kissed Helene at that birthday party when you were in Halifax.

You kissed Helene?

Yes, by a sink.

I kissed someone too. Or they kissed me.

In Halifax.

It was John. He wanted to change his suit. He asked me for my opinion. It was a mustard suit.

Where was I?

You were away.

I was reading.

We went there for a toke. He put on the jacket, picked up his fiddle, I could feel the fiddlehead pressed into my back.

Did you kiss him or did he kiss you.

Did you kiss Helene or did Helene kiss you?

I kissed Helene.

I can't believe you kissed Helene. I find her so unsexy.

Youre disappointed in my taste?

Well, you'll agree John's sexy.

Did you linger?

Look. It was like this.

Lydia turns, pretending she is John, and gives me a quick kiss. I press a knuckle into her back. She pauses to look at the kiss.

What are you doing.

Pressing a fiddlehead into your back.

He didnt do it intentionally. That hurt, by the way. So you didnt kiss Sandra.

No.

Okay, let's go to sleep now.

Okay.

I love you.

Okay.

I cross the constabulary parking lot with a basket of cheese scones. I am to meet Lydia at John and Agatha's.

There is a fire licking a short cement wall. It's a wild leaf fire. The flames are stretching up to a wooden fence above the wall. It's as if the leaves are transforming into flame. I pause before stamping it out. I'm considering a city gutted. I smother it with leaves and then stamp. The flames turn to smoke. I spread the leaves into a black stain on the sidewalk. Several new flames erupt. Then the heat leaves, a heat I hadnt felt, and the sidewalk is cold and boring.

I meet Lydia at the doorstep and for a moment we are strangers. We are edgy and excited. The door opens. John is wearing an apron. Agatha leans into us and says — what does she say? What she says sounds truthful to her and John. She is offering Lydia and me advice. They saw us through a teardrop window in the door. Saw our attempt to be new to each other.

Leo sits in a Canadian rocker. He changes seats with Sandra to be in it. It creaks. John: I bought that when Agatha was eight months pregnant with Harry.

He says this with a confidence. They have two children and a love for these children that supersedes personal hate.

There is a bowl of perogies and bacon. Sandra: Theyre fried. Lydia wants another before the bowl has gotten around. She doesnt realize it is going around. She reaches for it as John is peering into it. She hauls back her arm and laughs, and when John offers her the bowl she says no. He continues to coax her with the bowl. I try to imagine their kiss. I dont feel vulnerable about the kiss or how they are looking now. John is physically brilliant, and why deny Lydia this?

There are four bottles of red wine open. The strong green glass. A broken cork. Leo has broken it. He opened the bottle on the table. If he had put it between his knees and used leverage instead of just his wrist. His wrist broke it. Sandra is wearing orange. She says to me, studying my shirt, Purple. She lays a hand across my chest to feel my purple. There is a heat emanating off each finger. Leo says, You two would make a good couple, but he doesnt specify: me and Sandra? John and Lydia? Then John speaks to Agatha but not directly. She hands the sour cream to him, but he doesnt see it. She holds it slightly behind herself as he's at the stove with the last of the perogies, so she doesnt see that he doesnt see it. Agatha is giving off the air of familiarity with John. It is only because four seconds pass that she realizes. Then she places the cream on the corner of the table, where John can reach it. For four seconds she is still married to him. Table sounds like labia. There is not an ounce of meanness in anything.

Agatha: Leo, you sure like to wear red.

Lydia had said to John, Want help at the stove, John? but he walked past her to shake my hand. I guess not, she said.

This is my measurement of attention between John and Lydia.

Leo: I was taking pictures on the beach last night. The rocks and the snow, the waves, he says. Have you noticed the water? It's so cold and blue, like all the oxygen is squeezed out of it — like it's blood in the veins, just pure hydrogen up here in New-foundland.

Leo turns and his neck turns and he bends a little at the waist like a rooster and one hand is always twisting as if he's opening a door. Sandra's toes on my chair. Lydia has her ankle hooked on my calf and she's about to include Agatha on a thought. Sandra has asked what are the necessities.

Cigarettes, good coffee and art, she says.

Leo: Cigarettes and art.

Leo has a can of peas. Half a can for lunch, the other half for supper. He indicates the can of peas by making a C out of his middle finger and thumb. He eats them cold. He doesnt say, I dont heat them up. He says, I eat them cold. He was living in the van, then he rented an apartment that was right beside the van. He'd woken up and saw a ROOM FOR RENT sign in Greensville, South Carolina. The room is big enough to work in. The sink is used for developing. He pushes the bed in to the wall and works.

Sandra and Leo, I see, have been sleeping together.

There are two kids in the room above us, talking to girls on the phone and watching television and Sandra's toes are still clenching the edge of my chair. She is wearing black leggings and the knuckles of her toes are showing through white. Leo, pausing: Would it be okay if I took your picture, and he understands I'm thinking Sandra.

In bed. Me: They were sweet to each other.
Lydia: Well, they have two kids.

Leo says he's into contrived scenes. He likes being honest about things contrived.

He has a bottle of sambuca tucked in his armpit. Lydia says, Too bad there arent coffee beans.

She lights our glasses. She turns off the light.

I hesitate with flame circling the rim.

Lydia: You drink it down while it's aflame.

Are you sure.

Yes, it's how it's done.

I think I'm supposed to blow it out.

Just be fast and down it.

I feel a blue flame against my cheek. I try to drink quickly. The flame leaps into my mouth and Leo takes our picture. There is an audible sizzle near my eye. Lydia sets down her glass.

Leo: God, your eyebrow.

Is it bad?

Lydia: Does it hurt?

No.

Leo: It looks tender.

We stand in the rain, waiting. Leo lifts a lapel. He says, I guess we're getting wet. He has backed under Lydia's fire escape but it still drips. When he backs up he triggers the motion sensor on the porch light. He is bathed in artificial light.

Leo lifts his box of photographs. The rain and the porch light outlining him. He moves back under the stairs another foot and then sees the overhang on the garage. He points to it. And then Lydia, Sandra, are at the red door.

Lydia rubbed cocoa butter on my eye with her thumb.

Me: Youre my cornerman.

Yeah, I'm fixing your cut. Now go knock him out.

We drive everyone home. And then later, in bed, Lydia says, For a moment there, you looked like a fire-eater.

You convinced me I was.

Some of these stories were published in an earlier form: 'Something Practical' appeared in *The New Quarterly*. 'The Ground That Owns You' won the Newfoundland Arts & Letters Competition, was published in *Event* magazine, translated for *Antologia de cuentos canadienses contemporaneos* (Editorial Aldus, Mexico, 1996), and reprinted in *Melt Water* (Banff Press, 1999). 'The Pallbearer's Gloves' won the Newfoundland Arts & Letters Competition, was published in the *University of Windsor Review*, and reprinted in *Turn of the Story* (House of Anansi Press, 1999). 'Lustral' appeared in *Canadian Fiction Magazine*. 'Wormholes' was included in the anthology *Extremities: Fiction from the Burning Rock* (Killick Press, 1994). 'Femke, and His Then Girlfriend' was published in *Exile*; 'Lets Shake Hands Like the French' in the *Ottawa Citizen*. 'Diaphanous Is a Good Word for You' appeared in *The Malahat Review*.

Michael Winter was born in England and grew up in Newfoundland. He received a degree from Memorial University. His stories have appeared in most of this country's literary magazines, and been broadcast on national CBC radio. His work was selected for the anthologies *Best Canadian Stories '95*, *Melt Water* (Banff twenty-fifth anniversary collection, 1999), and *Turn of the Story* (House of Anansi Press, 1999). He has been translated into Spanish for a Mexican edition of Canadian fiction.

His first collection of stories, *Creaking in Their Skins*, appeared in 1994 (Quarry Press). A fictional memoir, *This All Happened*, was published in 2000 (House of Anansi Press).

Michael Winter lives in Toronto and St John's.